WOLF

THE NIGHTHAWK SERIES BOOK TWO

LISA LANG BLAKENEY

WRITERGIRL PRESS

COPYRIGHT

LISA LANG BLAKENEY

Love reading novels featuring hot alpha men who fall for smart women? Then join MY VIP MAILING LIST at http://LisaLangBlakeney.com/VIP and get a **free** book just for joining!

FOLLOW ME

Follow me on Facebook
Join my Fan Group
Follow me on Amazon
Follow me on Bookbub
Follow me on Instagram

LICENSE NOTE

This book is a work of fiction. Any similarity to real events, people, or places is entirely coincidental. All rights reserved. This book may not be reproduced or distributed in any format without the permission of the author, except in the case of brief quotations used for review.

The author acknowledges the trademarked status of products referred to in this book and acknowledges that trademarks have been used without permission.

This book contains mature content, including graphic sex. Please do not continue reading if you are under the age of 18 or if this type of content is disturbing to you.

This is a tribute to every little boy who ever made your heart skip a beat

The Masterson Series

Devour this addictive series about the possessive bad boy, Roman Masterson, who falls hard and fast for the girl he's promised his family to protect.

Masterson

Masterson Unleashed

Masterson In Love

Masterson Made

Joseph Loves Juliette

The King Brothers Series

Dive into this series of interconnected standalones featuring 3 alpha hot brothers and the women they lay claim to without apology.

Claimed - Camden & Jade

Indebted - Cutter & Sloan

Broken - Stone & Tiny

Promised - All King Brothers

The Nighthawk Series

Sexy & sweet sports romances set in the professional world of football. All standalones.

Saint - Saint & Sabrina

Wolf - Cooper & Ursula

Diesel - Mason & Olivia

Jett - Jett & Adrienne

Rush - Rush & Mia

The Valencia Mafia Series

Coming Soon. Get Notified!

MASTERSON

Meet Alpha Roman Masterson

Free For A Limited Time!

"Our passion is incredibly intense. The connection between us borders on the possessive. Our feelings are absolutely forbidden. The question now is…what the f*ck are we going to do about it?"

DOWNLOAD NOW

INTRODUCTION

From bestselling author, Lisa Lang Blakeney, comes a sweet and sexy STANDALONE football romance.

"A one-click, *damn I read it in one night*, boss romance and fated love story."

Ursula

My family thinks I'm crazy, my astrology chart says it's a mistake, but after three years of carefully molding the highly narcissistic Cooper Barnes into the athlete influencer of the year—I quit.

He won't care anyway. Whether they work for him or sleep with him, women have always been expendable to the billionaire baller. Even me.

Cooper

What in the ham sandwich is wrong with Ursula Owens? It's like she woke up one day this whole new person. A woman I don't recognize.

One day she was my quirky, highly organized assistant, happily managing my entire life for me. The next she is handing in her resignation with no warning and no reason.

I met her by chance, but I'm keeping her by choice. Maybe our love story is fated after all.

URSULA

I wake up entwined in sweaty cotton sheets that smell faintly of ocean breeze scented detergent, sweat, and fear. It's the third time this month that I've had the dream. Each one more vivid than the last. Each dream attempting to give me access to my vault of forgotten memories. Each attempt getting me only millimeters closer inside of my subconscious. To the pain. To the truth.

I was in the backseat by myself, strapped in tightly, and humming along to a radio block of seventies hits that my mother loved to listen to during long car rides. I remember kicking the back of her seat to the beat of the song, excited by how the lights on my sneakers lit up with every small punt.

I've never seen in my dreams exactly where we were coming from, but I know that we were on our way home from somewhere familiar. It was a route I'd been on countless times before. That I know for sure.

I knew we were getting closer to home as I began to see gargantuan steel buildings, hordes of people on foot, and beautiful green and silver confetti all over the streets. Remnants of a recent city parade. The light from each passing car would bounce off of the silver flecks of confetti spread across the black tar. This was a good memory. But in every iteration of the dream is the thunder.

Deafening, ear-splitting, soul-scarring thunder that was so frighteningly loud that it may have been the moment that I first believed in God. There was no other explanation for the source of such a sound. God was real, and he must have been very angry.

I felt terribly exposed sitting in a ninety-degree position directly behind my mother's seat. As if the thunder could reach out and touch us both and toss us into the Hudson River. I was afraid. So frightened that I unbuckled my seatbelt and folded myself in the space on the floor of the car between my seat and my mother's.

I remember feeling how odd it was that my mother wasn't frightened like me. She was still singing at the top of her lungs.

Billy Joel.

"Philadelphia Freedom."

And then we were spinning.

And then there was darkness.

CHAPTER ONE

URSULA

It's a picture perfect summer evening in Midtown, New York City. Warm enough to go strapless, but cool enough to still wear your hair down without it getting frizzy. Times Square is packed with tourists, the bars are packed with the locals, the bustling traffic is being policed by New York's finest, and you can just feel the energy crackling in the air.

It's palpable.

It's perfect.

In fact, this is the kind of night that makes working for the most narcissistic man I've ever met all worth it. We've got two important events on deck for tonight, and I've made sure to dot every *i* and cross every *t* in preparation for them, except I have uncharacteristically forgotten one important thing.

Shoes.

When I finally remembered that I didn't have a single decent pair to go with my scarlet red evening dress, I realized I only had three hours left to get ready. Yet thanks to my boss's trusty American Express black card, I was able to zip into Neiman Marcus and quickly buy a pair that works. Well ... they sort of work.

I am now the proud owner of a pair of brand new, seven hundred dollar, nude stilettos that miraculously elongate my stubby legs but hurt like all hell. I've come to the conclusion that whoever invented high heels was a man who hated women. I'd rather wear a pair of chucks any day.

"Hey, Courtney."

My phone is ringing off the hook today. Seems like every assistant in town is trying to secure a spot on our guest list.

"No, you should be fine for tonight. I've got you down for four in the VIP section. Just give the guy at the door your name. You're welcome."

Another call comes in as I wait for the car to pick me up.

"Hi, Millicent."

"Ursula, I had to make a few adjustments to the

seating at the last minute. Mr. Barnes is still in the first row of course, but I've shifted him and his parents, specifically, about five seats over and had to put the rest of you in the seats directly right behind him."

"He wanted the entire first row."

"I know but that doesn't work for the camera angles and all of that jazz. They wanted the seats all centered."

"What?"

That makes zero sense.

"I'm sorry but you know I don't make those decisions. The production team has a way of doing things that works for them. I just go with it."

I see my car pulling up and even with the slightly tinted windows, I can tell that my boss is already inside, so I need to end this conversation. It's my job to keep mistakes and missteps from him. All he wants to worry about is football. Nothing else.

"You know we don't like last minute changes, but I trust you, Millicent," I say quickly wrapping our call up. "I'll see you in a few."

"Thanks, love. See you in a few."

I try to hide it, but I can't help but grimace, as I painfully slide into the back seat of Coop's black SUV. His full-time driver, Tito, never misses anything and notices. He gives me an extended look of concern in the rearview mirror and then silently nods hello.

"Hey, Tito," I say with a smile and then I address my boss. "Hey, Coop."

Since he doesn't even acknowledge that I'm in the car (as per usual unless he's bitching), I decide to grab a moment of relief and slip my feet out of my heels. The structured leather of the shoes has already begun rubbing the back of my left ankle. Scraping it raw.

I'm in some pain, but I don't really have time for it. This is going to be another long night serving the man I work for. Tonight's "Athlete Influencer Of The Year" award winner—Cooper Barnes. Superstar tight end for The New York Nighthawk national football franchise, philanthropist, television personality and according to Forbes Magazine—one of the wealthiest men in America under the age of thirty.

This particular award is one he's wished and waited many years for, and tonight is a night that I've worked tirelessly to make happen.

Believe it or not, these awards aren't just randomly given out. The selection is not made by a committee but a group of his peers. So, you have to actually campaign for it, although you can't be blatant about it, and nobody "quietly" campaigned as hard for their athlete like I did for Coop.

I didn't just work this hard to get him this award because it's my job, but because it's my last hurrah. I want to go out with a bang. Leave my mark. Because once this night is over—I'm out of here.

I quit.

"What's up with the feet?" he asks me. Finally taking a moment to look away from his phone. A phone that drives him to complete distraction. All day, when he's not playing football, he checks texts, tweets, snapchats, Facebook, Instagram and any other form of social media that may make mention of him on a daily basis. Funny how he rarely uses the thing to actually talk to people.

"They hurt." *Obviously.*

He raises an eyebrow at my response but not out of concern. I'm sure that he's thinking that somehow my sore feet are going to affect his big night—a night that I had everything in the world to do with making happen for him by the way—and he doesn't like it, not one bit.

"Relax," I offer before he says something that's going to make me want to karate chop his neck. "I'm going to run into the store and grab a Band-Aid and some Neosporin."

"How long is that going to take?"

I roll my eyes (to myself of course) then plaster on one of my trademark smiles. I've used this smile for the last three years to get through many tough days as Coop's assistant.

"Five minutes tops. You won't be late. You can start walking the red carpet while I fix myself up in the car."

Coop places his phone down in the space in between us, looks at me with determined eyes, then to Tito.

"Pull over."

CHAPTER TWO

URSULA

"You are my date for this event, Owens. I can't walk the red carpet without you."

I hate that I almost blush when Coop says the word *date*. He says it in that signature deep and demanding voice of his. The voice that makes every man want to fight him and every woman shiver way down deep in her panties. He's entirely too sexy for his own good, and it's even worse because he knows it.

I had to admit to myself long ago that while there's nothing I can do about my indefensible attraction to Coop, there's also nothing that I'd ever want to do about it. I know the man better than most people on this planet, and from what I've learned about him over the last three years, he is the last guy on earth that any woman should get involved with—at least not with her heart.

This attraction or whatever you'd like to call it isn't even something that I feel all of the time. Most times I don't even give him a second glance, but occasionally he may say or do something in a way that makes me catch my breath for a moment. The tone of his voice. A smile he may give me. The feeling is fleeting though and then I totally forget that it ever happened, which is why I've never bothered to mention it to anyone including my sisters. God knows that they'd make way more out of it than it is or ever would be.

"No one is going to care if your assistant takes a few minutes to catch up," I say. "The media and the fans are all here to see you. It's only important that you get out there on time. Not me."

"I fucking care."

For some reason tonight those three words rattle me. Maybe it's because this is such a huge night for Coop, and I'm feeling a little sentimental, or maybe it's because I know I'm going to be quitting soon and I feel a little guilty.

Wait a minute though. I know better than to be shaken by his empty declaration. This isn't about him genuinely *caring,* or desiring my company, or giving me the chance to enjoy a night that I spent a lot of time making happen. This is solely about him not wanting to show up to the biggest night of his career alone.

It's been almost six weeks since Coop dumped his latest flavor of the month, Megan Ross. I didn't think the woman had much substance, but I guess good conversation doesn't matter when you're a popular Instagram model with a huge butt, fake breasts, and over five million followers. In fact, I'm pretty sure that the two of them didn't do too much talking at all.

I've attended public events with Coop before, but we've never strolled the red carpet together. It's clear though that he's dragging me along as his "date" to show Megan or maybe even to show the world that he's fine without her. In my opinion, he's trying too hard. Everyone knows he doesn't do anything serious.

"You're doing too much," I say.

"What did you say to me?" he asks in a steely cold voice. Once upon a time that voice used to make me shiver and shake in fear, but that's no longer the case. I've since learned that it's just one of Coop's many strategic tools to keep people at a distance or to control them.

He uses his size, his voice, and sometimes his coldness to intimidate his opponents on the field and in business, but it doesn't work anymore on this girl here. I know better.

"I *said* that you're going through an awful lot to prove that you're over some woman that *you* dumped by the way. It's pitiful. If you miss Megan so much, just tell her you made a mistake. Get back together. I'm sure she'll jump at the chance."

"You think this is about Megan?"

"What else would it be about?"

"We were never serious. This isn't about her."

"Of course, it wasn't serious, but whatever this is about, I think it would be smarter if I didn't walk the red carpet with you. Just so there won't be any misunderstandings."

"Such as?"

"Such as Megan and whoever else thinking that I'm actually *with* you tonight. This is a big night for you. Other than the Super Bowl, I'd say that it's the biggest night. Some people might jump to the wrong conclusions."

I've been able to be mostly anonymous the entire time I've worked for Coop. The woman behind the man. I really don't want any permanent reminders of me being connected to this night on camera, on tape, or anywhere. I want a clean break.

"You've been working for me for three years and

have been to every game, every publicity event, and every interview I've ever agreed to. The people that matter already know that you're just my assistant."

Just.

I hate that word.

It's fine though. I just have to hang in there a little longer, and then I'm done with all of this.

"Exactly," I say brightly, shaking off his condescending remark. "We're basically saying the same thing. Everybody knows that I'm not your real date, so why do we need to walk in together and make it appear as if we are?"

Coop lazily looks me up and then down, and then his eyes settle on my cleavage—what little of it there is —for a moment before he speaks.

"The red looks good on you, Owens."

I stumble to come back with a quick response. Coop *never* pays me a compliment. Tito notices it too. He's smirking up front and seems to be taking an unusual pleasure in our exchange tonight. I'll have to speak to him later about doing a better job of minding his own business.

I swallow the lump in my throat and manage to retort with a respectful, "Thank you, Coop."

"Tito, let's stop at the next pharmacy and get a first aid kit. We should always have one in the car anyway.

We'll wait for Owens to repair her ankle, and then we'll walk the carpet together as planned."

"Gotcha, boss."

"But—" I protest.

"You know I don't like talking to every sports journalist and blogger on the planet. That's your job. It's my job to put on some shades, look good, and pose for a few photos."

"You're being unreasonable."

"We walk in together. End of story."

Then he picks up his phone and starts typing furiously. I know what that means. Our conversation is unceremoniously over, and I'm simply going to have to dig deep tonight and do my job.

Thankfully, it's one of the last orders he'll ever give me.

CHAPTER THREE

URSULA

I've attended a ton of red carpet events before, but for some reason tonight, I'm tense. Maybe because my ankle mishap feels like the start of some bad omen. So, after cleaning up my wound, I take the liberty of cracking open a bottle of Prosecco from Coop's stash and take a huge swig straight from the bottle.

It's probably one of the most unprofessional things I've ever done, but my excuse is that I'm using it to swallow two ibuprofen gel caps and to quash the uneasiness that's starting to bloom in the pit of my stomach.

The night has barely begun and already I have an

injury, I've had a few choice words with Coop, and I've been texting the deejay I hired for the afterparty and have received zero response. He should be running a sound check right now, and so far, he's a complete no show.

Simply craptastic.

I suddenly feel the stares of both men in the car.

"What?!" I blurt out.

"You all right?" Coop asks staring at the bottle in my hand. "You know we have plenty of bottled water in here."

"I needed something a little stronger to dull the pain. Sue me."

"Seriously? You're acting like you broke your collarbone or something. Talk to me about pain when you've lived through something like that."

"It's rare to find a man so proud of *everything* he's ever done. Even when he breaks a bone getting pulverized on the football field. Isn't your job *not* to get hit?"

"Make light of it if you want, but they pay me the Benjamins, because I can take a hit or two without crying about it."

"I know. I know. Your pain threshold is the highest in the land. You're like the bravest gladiator *ever* to have fought on the field of battle." I roll my eyes for effect. "But how about you come talk to me when you play football in a pair of brand new stilettos. Now that I'd love to see."

Coop snickers. "Are you drunk off of that one gulp of Prosecco or something?"

"What?! No."

"Highest pain threshold *in the land*. Who talks like that? And gladiators fight in a ring, not a battlefield."

"Whatever."

Tito is chuckling to himself up front.

I make sure to cut my eyes at him.

"All I'm saying is that was an expensive bottle of wine to crack open just to take a couple of pills. Right, Tito?"

"A bottle that you just had lying around the car," I protest.

"To celebrate *my* big night, not yours."

Touché.

"True ... well ... Tito can replace it while we're in the show. I'll pay for it, of course."

"Pay for it?" Coop snickers. "You're missing the point, but I'm going to let it slide tonight because for some reason I think you're more nervous about me getting this damn award than I am. I've never seen you this ... off your game."

I hurt my ankle and I'm off my game? I take a swig

of sparkling wine and I'm off my game? That's an exaggeration if ever I've heard one. I'm never off my game. I have been scheduling and running Coop's entire life for the last three years without incident. Okay ... maybe that's not exactly true. In the beginning I stunk at this job. I was totally unqualified and scared to death, but I'm fucking fantastic at it now. The nerve of him.

Before I have a chance to respond to Coop's totally inaccurate observation of me, Tito pulls up in front of Madison Square Garden. We're here. The awards ceremony is being held in the small theater inside The Garden and will be broadcast live to millions of sports fans across the nation.

The sidewalks are teeming with paparazzi and fans, but Coop doesn't like to ride around in obnoxiously expensive cars like some of his contemporaries. No one knows that it's him in the car, because it is so nondescript. Just a plain black Chevy Tahoe with slightly tinted windows and a few bells and whistles on the inside like a mini bar.

I text Millicent to let her know that we've arrived. She instructs me to have Tito pull around to the side of The Garden, so that she can give me our passes before we hit the red carpet. I will be in charge of making sure Coop's family gets into their seats while he gives a couple of the obligatory interviews and photos on the red carpet. The same interviews that he thinks he's not doing, but that I've promised he would as long as they give us something in return. Their return is usually a cover or a free ad spot for his nonprofit organization.

In between all of that, I have to make sure that the afterparty he's throwing in partnership with our corporate sponsor goes off without a hitch. Obviously, a large company like Nike has a huge event planning department for things like this, but Coop demands a personal touch, aka me, when he throws an event. There will be a lot of celebrities attending, and he wants to make sure that it's a party that goes down in the record books. A party that everyone will still be talking about for years to come.

Since the bottle is open, I say the hell with it and take another swig of Prosecco and then get to work.

"Stay inside," I order Coop. "I need to pop out and get the passes."

"I thought your feet hurt."

"I'm fine now."

He firmly pushes his hand down on my left thigh, and it sends an immediate shock to my core. I can count on one hand the number of times that Coop and I have had physical contact. This makes the sixth time.

"Text whoever is in charge tonight and tell them to bring the passes to the car."

I don't dare move a muscle.

Honestly, I can't move.

My dress is simple; a sexy red, strapless gown made from a soft jersey fabric with a huge slit on the side. I can feel everything through this dress.

The warmth of his hand.

The texture of his skin.

The cool metal of the Super Bowl ring around his finger.

"Well, are you going to do what I told you or not?"

He's staring at me as if I've lost every bit of good sense that I have left. I think I have. If I hold my breath any longer I might just pass out.

"Could you—?"

"Could I what?"

"Could you move your hand, so I can grab my purse, please?"

I hope he hasn't figured out that his touch had any sort of effect on me.

"Hand lifted, Owens."

One little corner of Coop's mouth turns up into a devilish smirk.

Crap sandwich, I think he noticed.

URSULA

The life of an assistant is hectic, and you're bound to make a mistake, especially when you're dealing with the egos of athletes, which is exactly why I don't want to bother Millicent any more than I have to. While I work hard for my one football ego, she has to manage hundreds of them tonight, so it's going to take every bit of strength I have not to pull her to the side and berate her like I want to at this moment.

"Hey, Ursula. Wow! You look nice when you want to, huh? I don't think I've ever seen you dressed in anything but Converse and skinny jeans."

I take a deep breath and plaster on one of my fake

smiles. One thing you can't teach a person no matter how much money they make is how to have class. You either have it or you don't.

"Nice to see you too, Megan. Are you looking for Coop?"

I crane my neck around to see if I can locate him in the lobby teemed with athletes from all over the world.

"Oh no, girl. I'm here with Paul Parinzino."

Megan smiles like a cat who just swallowed a canary.

"I saw you standing over here and just wanted to say hi."

I'm dumbfounded. I don't know Megan that well, in fact, I don't know her at all because she and Coop dated briefly, but I wouldn't have guessed that she would do something this low.

Paul Parinzino is the brand new rookie the Nighthawks have drafted as Saint Stevenson's backup quarterback. He's probably young and dumb and thinks someone like Megan is his dream woman, but he also has to know that she was sleeping with Coop literally a few weeks ago. I mean, he must know that. She posted about it every ten seconds on Instagram.

"Well, uh, you have a good time tonight, Megan. I need to get back to work."

After we exchange a few more very bogus

pleasantries, it only takes a second for me to realize that we both are headed in the same direction, same seating section, and the same row where Coop's family are already seated.

"Hello, Mrs. Barnes," she addresses Coop's mother. Coop's father must have stepped out for a moment. "I'm a really good friend of your son's."

Megan extends her arm out for a handshake.

Wowza, she's so shameless.

"And this is Paul Parinzino, future star quarterback of The Nighthawks."

Parinzino looks uncomfortable but shakes Mrs. Barnes' hand too. "Nice to meet you."

After the two of them take their seats, Mrs. Barnes uses her pointer finger to motion for me to bend down so she can whisper something to me.

"Did you know about this, Ursula?"

"What do you mean, Mrs. Barnes?"

"I know exactly who she is. Why is she sitting next to Coop?"

I knew I felt a bad omen coming on.

"I apologize, Mrs. Barnes. I'll take care of it."

To add more bad juju on the night, not only is Megan on the arm of the newly signed rookie quarterback from Coop's team but sitting on the other side of his seat is player, Peter Duncan, from a rival team that Coop has had a long running war of words with.

Granted—Duncan is a NFL veteran with three Super Bowl rings and a legendary career, but there were a lot of other places they could have seated him on Coop's big night. Frankly, I think the network did this for ratings. In a world of seedy reality television, I feel like almost anything goes these days.

I scan the room to look for Millicent, when I finally spot her standing by the sound booth. Before I walk toward her, I feel a sturdy hand grab my wrist.

"Wait."

The seventh instance of physical contact.

"What's up, Coop?" I ask clearing my throat.

"You were about to find the showrunner, right?"

"Yes."

"Don't change anything. Nothing can ruin my night."

Coop's father who's standing right behind him agrees.

"That's right, son. Be the bigger man."

"But, Coop—"

"I'm the star of this shit show, so we're going to sit down and enjoy every moment of it. Megan and Duncan are unimportant. They don't matter."

Coop's mother chimes in, "I think you should let

Ursula do her job and fix this. Serves them right to get their seats moved. Shame on Megan. Good thing you never brought her to my house for dinner."

"Ursula did her job, Mom." *Wait, did he just defend me?* "It's just the network fucking with us for ratings. I won't give them the satisfaction."

Coop and his father exchange a knowing look then Mr. Barnes sits down next to his wife. "Come on, Ann. This is Coop's decision, and frankly I'm in total agreement. Fuck 'em."

Coop's mom finally acquiesces. "Okay, then. Fuck 'em."

Sheesh, the whole family has potty mouths.

While they sabotaged our seating, the network made up for it during the actual ceremony. It was truly a testimony to how respected Coop is, that so many athletes and other celebrities were either live on stage or pre-recorded a video saying nice things about Coop.

He makes me a better player, because he is the best.

If I want to see an example of excellence I watch him play.

Mr. Friday Night Lights!

His commitment to educating our children is unprecedented.

The funniest man I've ever met.

Cockiest player on the playing field.

Kindest man on the planet.

I wasn't sure where they dug up all these people, because I've been around Coop almost around the clock for three years, and he is definitely a loner. When did he find the time to make these sorts of connections with people? Connections that would inspire them to make these comments. Perhaps like a television drama, the ceremony was all scripted.

I don't know, but it doesn't matter. Even with Megan rolling her eyes at him all night, he left the ceremony on a high, and we'll be sure to continue the celebration at the afterparty even if I have to deejay the dang party myself. I'm going to go out with a bang even if it kills me.

URSULA

"Gutterball!"

My sisters both brazenly high five each other as they cackle. Carla, the pregnant one, stuffs a few french fries in her mouth as she grins in triumph; while Monica pops a wad of Double Bubble in her mouth and then practically bulldozes me out of the bowling lane with her voluptuous hips.

"My turn!" she exclaims.

They're both so ridiculously jubilant, because I just rolled a gutterball for my team—the team being me and our seventy-five-year old grandmother. I shake my head in disbelief. These two have no shame when it comes to competitive sports.

"It's pretty sad when you get *this* excited about beating your Nana on bowling night," I say scornfully.

My words don't seem to faze either one of them. Self-satisfying smirks are still plastered across their faces.

"Speak for yourself," Nana blurts out from behind me. "I haven't thrown a gutterball like you just did since 1978. Your sisters didn't beat me, they beat you."

"That's right, Nana!" My sisters roar with laughter. "You tell her."

I make a pouty face and sit back over on the side bench.

Nana is a turncoat.

"So, tell us about Mr. Wonderful, Ursula. How's that gorgeous man doing?"

My sister Monica and probably half of the women in this city have a celebrity crush on Coop.

"Funny that you mention him."

"Yeah—what is it? Do you have some tea on him?"

Both of my sisters are practically salivating at the mouth. They think I'm going to break my confidentiality clause and tell them some sort of juicy gossip (also known as the tea) about Coop. They're so predictable. They've been dying for me to spill the beans on him for years. I never do. I never would. It's against my confidentiality clause and more importantly my moral compass.

"Is he really seeing Ariana Grande?"

"No."

They don't listen to me.

"Ooh yeah—is he, Ursula? I mean she's so young."

"No," I say again with emphasis.

"Totally too young for him and way too skinny. Plus, they're not a good match. She's a Cancer and Coop's an Aquarius."

"Is she a June or July Cancer?"

"She's June."

"Ewww."

Seriously?

"Yeah, those late June Cancers are the worst, but I think her voice makes up for it. That girl can really sing."

"Yep, that's true she can, but your butt looks way better than hers."

"Does it? Thanks, sis. I've been using this squat press thing at the gym and—"

I hold my hand up to stop them both from their incessant chatter and to finally share my big news.

"I'm quitting my job."

Suddenly three sets of jolted eyes are on me.

"WHAT?!" they exclaim.

"You can't do that," my sister Carla says. "I won't let you do that."

"I can, and I am," I say defiantly.

"What on earth for? You have a dream job. People would die for that job. You get to hang around that beautiful specimen of a man and get paid handsomely for it."

"Yeah and aren't you like the big kahuna at your job? I've overheard you on some of your work calls. Don't you tell his other employees what to do? Didn't you have a big hand in his big awards night?"

"Not to mention that you get to make your own hours. When you're getting a blow out at the hairdresser's in the middle of the freakin' day, I'm carrying a heavy mailbag and running from vicious Pomeranians."

"I might pay to see that one day. You running from a dog as big as the size of your head," Carla jokes.

"First of all, I never go to the hairdressers during work hours. I barely go at all."

"That's obvious," adds Nana, giving her unwanted two cents about my lack of style.

I ignore her and continue. "And it isn't that I'm a big kahuna or tell his employees what to do," I say. "But it's more like I'm the gatekeeper. I maintain his complicated schedule. Between football and his business ventures, things can get complicated, so he prefers for people to go through me to get to him. My daily grind is making sure that I don't muck up his day. I have to triple check dates, times, and orders."

"Sounds like the perfect job to me, especially because you're good as hell at it. I know you didn't grow up saying you'd make a kick-ass executive assistant one day, but here you are, doing the damn thing."

"And doing it well!"

"Yep, if you don't want that job then I'll take it. It beats working at the post office."

"There's no perfect job, Monica."

"That's exactly what I'm saying. We're basically in agreement. Why are you searching for something that doesn't exist when you've got a sweet gig already?"

"There's nothing wrong with my job, per se, other than the fact that my boss has the inability to think about anyone other than himself, but that's not really the point. I could live with that if I really wanted to. What I'm actually saying is that it's the only real job I've ever had. The only thing I've done since college. I want to try something else. Explore my options and maybe find my passion."

"Passion?"

"Puh-lease ... passion is overrated."

"And are you going to just hop from dead end job to dead end job trying to find yourself? What do you mean exactly by exploring your options and finding your passion?"

Carla is the oldest and sometimes flip flops between acting like my sister and acting like my mother. She's questioned every big decision I've ever made, and I am always seeking her approval.

"Yeah, sis, we don't get it. You work for a gorgeous man. A football player. A self-made billionaire. What better options are there?" Monica agrees.

"I want to do something else. Something different," I say emphatically, frustrated that they aren't telling me what a great decision I've made. "Something unlike what I'm doing."

"Unlike working for a *god*?"

"Working for a narcissist," I correct Monica.

"You mean working for those washboard abs and those tree trunk legs."

"And that butt!"

"Ugh, you guys are hopeless and gross."

"Oh, and don't forget about that killer smile of his."

"And that laugh. What about his laugh?"

"Oh, right. His teeth are the perfect shade of arctic

white. I bet he gets them professionally bleached, doesn't he, Ursula?"

"As if I'd tell either of you," I say finally getting a word in edgewise.

"Why not? Inquiring minds want to know."

"Would you two stop it?" I chastise. "You are the main people in my life who always complain that I never have any time for anything."

"We said that?" they ask in unison.

"Yes, you." I point directly at them. "Monica, you always say I'm a disgrace to millennials everywhere, because I can't hang out for a drink on a random Thursday night with you."

"She's right. You never give anyone any notice, and you do always want to do something on a Thursday," Carla chimes in. "It's weird."

"And Carla, you've been passive aggressively threatening me with that baby inside of your tummy since it's conception. What was the last thing you said? Something about how you hope the baby will be able to recognize my face since I never come over to your house."

"Ooh that's true. You do say that, Carla."

"Babies need repetition to recognize faces," Carla declares. "That's just the facts."

Nana has been sitting quietly sipping on her can of

diet green tea ginger ale, but at this point decides to jump into the conversation.

"The real issue here is that if you leave that job, somebody else is going to snatch up that man."

"Sure will."

"Wait ... what?"

Carla and I look at Monica and Nana like they've lost their minds.

"Snatch him up? How about if I leave my job, then maybe someone will finally *snatch me up* and make an honest woman out of me. I could never date anyone working for that tyrant. No one would put up with my erratic late night schedule. Always being at his beck and call. I'm twenty-four years old, and I've never had a real relationship."

"You haven't met the right person because you already work for him."

"Nana, you are so off base. There is nothing between Coop and me. He's like the big brother that I never wanted. There is nothing between us. Zero. Zilch. Nada."

Nana lifts her eyes up slowly from behind her can of soda. "Touchy. Touchy."

Monica giggles. "Can I just say that I think that *tyrant* is too strong of a word to use to describe that wonderful man you work for?"

"You don't know him."

"Well now that you've brought it up, you're right we don't. You won't let us get to know him. You've been keeping us away from him for three years with all of your excuses. It's embarrassing when our friends ask us what Cooper Barnes is like, and we're forced to tell them that we've never met the man. Are we your ugly stepsisters or something? Are you embarrassed by us, Cinderella?" Monica asks with her hands firmly planted on her hips.

Monica and Carla are indeed my older stepsisters, but they're far from ugly, and they could never embarrass me. In fact, these two are awesome women, my best friends, and probably the best thing to ever happen to me since the accident.

CHAPTER SIX

URSULA

Memories of the accident come to me in flashes at random times and in cold sweats. It was a rainy late night in March, and I was only six years old. I remember it was March because the city was still cleaning up after the big St. Patrick's Day parade, and there was green confetti everywhere. I thought it was so pretty.

According to the stories I've heard over the years, my mother was driving a little too fast and the driver of the car that hit us may have had a few too many beers. Although I have frequent nightmares about that night, I don't remember details. I don't remember enough.

All I know for sure is what I was told. That

someone hit us and then we rolled over about three times causing a five-car collision behind us, and ending upside down on the side of FDR drive. I'm not sure exactly how, but I made it out alive albeit bruised and battered. My mother didn't make it out at all.

My stepmother, Evelyn, was a friend of the family who respectfully supported us through that difficult time, and then about two years after the accident, married my father, and the five of us have been a happy family ever since.

Sure, there were some bumps along the road, but there isn't one day that I'm not grateful that God put them in my life right when I so desperately needed family. Even Nana is good to me. She's Monica and Carla's biological grandmother but treats me exactly the same, if not even a little better at times.

Carla and Monica took their roles as my big sisters seriously. As a tradition, every year they would give me a bag of Swedish Fish candy on my first day of school with a handwritten note. Even senior year, they continued to fight my battles; they gave a wedgie to this one boy who was bullying me. They've always frightened my boyfriends; that's why I've never had a half decent one, and they could always make me laugh. No biological sister could have treated me any better. I adore them.

"You really should be thanking me. I've saved you a huge amount of disappointment. This fantasy you've created around who you think Coop is would have been completely obliterated."

"I don't care what you say, Urs. That man didn't win this year's Influencer Athlete Award for nothing. You heard what all of those people said about him. He's a phenomenal player, he does so much for the community, and he's well respected. There's no way that he can be as bad as you say. You might want to take a moment and think about all of that before making the final decision to quit the best job you'll ever have."

I'm disappointed that they aren't excited for me, but I don't bother challenging my sister's warped opinion of my boss anymore. It's my fault. I make him look good. I've made what I do look easy. I have calculated and executed Coop's every want and wish for the last three years.

I know how to squash drama, how to massage the media's coverage of him, how to ignore his egotistical comments and how to make him the perfect protein smoothie. I'm sure to most people it looks like I have a dream job but being an assistant to one of the most self-loving, highly opinionated players in the league is not for the faint of heart. You need thick skin. Elephant skin. Rhinoceros skin.

"Think about it this way. I've saved enough money that I can literally take off a year and help you with the baby while I figure out what my next move is."

Carla's eyes enlarge. Now, that's an idea that she can get excited about.

"And on the weekends when Dexter is home with Carla and the baby, I can hang with you, Monica. We can order tequila shots all night and get twisted out of our minds if you want. Why? Because I won't have to worry about being sober twenty-four hours a day just in case *he* calls me for something. Don't you get it? I'm free now."

I twirl around like a ballerina.

An awkward ballerina holding a bowling ball.

"Ursula Owens, I don't want to hear anything about you getting *twisted*."

I cringe a bit at Nana's reprimanding tone. I don't like to disappoint her either, but she should face the truth at some point. Adults drink alcohol. Including me. It's crazy how they all still see me as the baby.

"Sorry, Nana, but I haven't done any of the things that women in their twenties do because of this job. It's a rite of passage for me to get drunk and party once in a while, and I didn't do it while I was in college. Not really. I was too worried about keeping my scholarship to party."

I was an acting major in the fine arts department, and because I had a major role in every theater production at my high school and because my stepmom dutifully pays her tithes; our church awarded their annual "full ride" scholarship to me. The only thing I had to make sure to do was to keep my GPA up.

The look on my family's face when I was awarded it was not only filled with pride but loaded with pressure. Neither of my sisters have degrees. Monica went to a community college for a year and then quit to work at the post office, and Carla married Dexter young and does medical billing from home. I was expected to go to school, do well, and most of all graduate with a degree. There was no room for failure.

"She's right," Monica concedes. "This job has been her whole life."

"But look at what she has to show for it," Nana says. "She's traveled all over the country and even overseas. She has money in the bank. A nice apartment. That's way more than I even dreamed of having at her age."

"But ..." I use my fingers to make a point of listing the drawbacks of my job. "No friends. No pets. No boyfriend. No auditions."

"No debt. No moochers. No whiny husbands. No dog hair in your bed," Carla counters. "But let's not play the game of whose grass is greener on the other side. Dexter and I are fighting to make ends meet and we are both working. In my opinion, this just doesn't seem like the right time to make such a risky move."

"I've got quite a bit saved," I say with a bit of a cocky tone.

"Ooh, someone's bragging." Carla takes a light swat at my butt.

"Well it sounds like you've made your decision," Monica interjects. "When are you going to tell him? How are you going to tell him? I imagine it won't go very well, if you remember that I've overheard some of your phone conversations, and you two don't seem to have a normal boss and employee relationship. You guys, I don't know, play around a lot. And he seems extremely ... dependent on you."

"I'm going to tell him this week. I just have to tighten up a few things I'm apart of with his foundation before I go."

"Oh yeah, he's opening that school for boys in September, right?"

"Yes."

"Why would you leave before he opens the school? That seems kind of a big deal."

"There's never going to be a good time to leave," I say defensively. "He always has something important coming up. I want to do it now because it just seems like the right time to do it."

"You mean before you lose your nerve."

"No, that's not what I mean at all." I sigh in exasperation.

"Are you a hundred percent sure about this?" Carla asks with concern.

"Trust me, when I tell him, he'll be fine. He's always saying that *everyone is expendable and replaceable*." I mimic Coop's deep voice. "He's not going to care as much as you all seem to think he will."

"Speaking of the awards ... that after party was killer. Thanks for the invite, baby sis."

"You're welcome."

Carla sticks out her tongue at us. "Boo, I should have been the plus one."

"You can't drink. You can't dance. What would have been the point of you going?" Monica says dismissively. "You would have been like a wet blanket."

"You should be on bed rest anyway," I add. "You shouldn't be out partying and to be honest—not bowling either."

"You're just mad because you're losing."

"I'm thinking of the health of my future niece or nephew."

"Well I couldn't sit in the house another damn minute. Nana said it would be good for me and the baby to get out and move our bodies. Didn't you, Nana?"

Carla has already had two difficult pregnancies that resulted in late miscarriages. We're all being extra cautious about this pregnancy. Some of us are being more cautious than others. In fact, my brother-in-law, Dexter, would probably kill us all if he knew we were out bowling instead of in the house watching *CSI* reruns like Carla told him we were.

"Last time I checked, Nana wasn't a doctor," I say.

"You've never even had sex! What do you know?"

Nana sips on her ginger ale and then speaks. "I've given birth three times, and I know what I know. The baby needs movement. A little bowling won't put Carla into early labor. The baby will decide when he or she wants to arrive."

"I'm not saying she shouldn't get out of the house, but she probably shouldn't be exerting herself."

"No need to argue about it now. She's here, she's playing, and we're not taking her home. I don't consider bowling an aerobic sport."

"Thank you, Doctor Monica." I'm staying out of it at this point.

"And now that we've unsuccessfully talked you out of making the biggest mistake of your life, Ursula, can we finish whipping your butt?" Monica asks, adding a little levity back into the afternoon.

"Let's do it," I say rubbing my hands together like a praying mantis. "I'm feeling lucky. I'm going to quit my job, I'm about to roll a strike, and my life is going to be awesome from here on out. I don't care what ya'll say."

"Okay, Ursula!"

"You've got this."

"Roll that strike, sweetie," Nana cheers.

And then ...

Gutterball.

COOP

"Can I get you anything else, Mr. Barnes? How about a little more pie?"

The question just posed to me wouldn't be so annoying if it hadn't been laced with sexual innuendo. I suppose it makes complete sense though, because the woman asking is flashing the biggest areolas I've ever seen in my life. Pert nipples that are begging to be tweaked or tugged as they overtly jut through a transparent white tank top. Their state no doubt manipulated by the frigid conditions of the room and torrid thoughts of me.

I can't help but stare at them for a moment before finally looking away. I love the shape and form of a woman, of all women, but I want no parts of this one. She's trouble. Paternity court type of trouble.

"Nah, I'm good."

I'm sitting on a stool, on a freezing set, in front of bright lights and a green screen, getting ready to shoot my third laundry detergent commercial for Bolt detergent—my latest endorsement deal. One of the executives for the company, Brad, was my college roommate, and I owed him one, so I agreed to the deal. When we were freshmen I yacked in his mom's brand new Toyota on our way home from a frat party, and he's never let me forget it. I've been "owing him one" ever since.

I've just finished filling myself up on a variety of crap from the craft service table. A table where Miss perky nipples was serving up dessert. I'm supposed to be cutting out all refined sugars and white flour from my diet. It's the strict nutrition regimen I stick to when I'm getting ready for the season, but the mini pecan pies on the table were calling me. Pecan pie always reminds me of home.

"You certainly are *good*, Mr. Barnes." She pretends to brush crumbs off of her chest to draw even more attention to her breasts. "Good in every way."

Oh, for fuck's sake. Where is Owens? It's my assistant's job to keep these kind of desperate women from approaching me. It's not like her to be late or a no-show. I text her a couple of angry emojis. Words aren't necessary. She's been like my right hand man and little sister combined for the last three years. She knows me best. She'll get the point.

Me: :(

Huh, usually she responds right away.

"You're amazing on the football field." The woman continues talking. Distracting me from my angry texting. "I love to watch you throw the ball."

See what I mean? She's clueless. I don't throw shit. That's not what a tight end does.

"So, you're a football fan?"

"Absolutely!"

Not.

"Who's your favorite player?"

There's no way this woman knows anything about the game of professional football. I can smell a real fan a mile away, and all I smell on her is a knockoff version of Chanel #5 and desperation.

"You of course."

How did I know?

"So, you like winners then."

I wink at her totally realizing that I shouldn't be encouraging this woman, but sometimes I'm an ass when I'm bored or annoyed.

"Absolutely."

The woman's eyes grow hungry and move lower toward my nether regions. While she is fairly attractive, and she's making her intentions crystal clear, I'm simply not interested.

For one, I'm not a kid anymore, and I don't sleep with just any random woman—especially since the season is starting up. That's a lawsuit waiting to happen. And two, she would just be too easy. I can tell that if I asked her to suck me off in front of the entire set that she probably would. Not that I would ask. My mother raised me better than that.

"Thanks for the pie and the personal attention but duty calls."

I turn myself around on the stool with my back toward her to finally put this conversation to rest.

"Wait, Cooper, I want to give you my number."

Is there anything I just said in the last five minutes to make this woman think that I would want to keep in touch? Or that she could address me using my first fucking name?

"No thank you."

"I can make you more pecan pie or you know—" She tries to give me a sultry look. "Whatever you have a taste for."

"No. Thank. You."

Can I make myself any clearer, captain obvious?

"Did I misread the signals when you were over at the table earlier?" she asks almost as if she's offended. Angry even.

"When I thanked you for the plate of pie and the extra napkin?" I ask in disbelief.

"I thought we made a connection."

"Over dessert?" I snicker.

"Excuse me? Are you laughing at me?"

"Sorry, darlin', but there's no pie in the world that would make me want your phone number."

At this point it's pretty obvious that this woman is considering hitting me across the head with the stainless steel spatula that she's holding. She would never be fast enough to succeed, but I guess Owens believes she can, because she's making a beeline for us from clear across the room.

"Are we okay here?" she asks stepping in between us with her saccharin sweet voice.

"Oh, you finally arrived?" I say to her.

"Are we okay here?" she asks a little more icily this time.

"Of course, we are," I respond with little affect. "Why wouldn't we be?"

Finished with this conversation, I go back to my

meaningless text war with my agent. I've got a list of people on my shit list today.

"Miss?" Owens addresses crazy nipples. "Are you with craft services?"

"Yes, I am."

"Well I know the owner of the company personally, and I will be sure to tell her what great service you have provided today. Mr. Barnes is quite particular about what he eats, and I see he has an empty plate over there. It must have been delicious."

"It was crap," I say without looking up. Irritated that Owens thinks she has to smooth things over with this intrusive woman. I was minding my own business when she barged into my personal space. Connection my ass. She just wants her bills paid.

"Did you just say my mother's food tasted like crap?" she asks incredulously. Her face contorted into the ugliest expression.

Fuck me. This is just my luck. Of course, it's this woman's mother who is the owner of the catering company.

"You're incredibly rude," she continues berating me. "I guess everything I've read about you is true."

Owens's large doe-like eyes squeeze tightly closed in frustration.

"I'm almost positive that it is not what Mr. Barnes

meant. Right, sir?" She darts those angry doe eyes of hers at me.

"Well as a matter of fact—" Owens quickly quiets me with a purposeful elbow to the stomach. "Umph."

"I didn't realize that Stephanie had children who worked in the business. Private Plates Catering always provides an array of delicious choices for us. Please tell her that."

"You don't have to kiss my ass, Miss whoever you are. It's a little too late for that."

Sometimes I can be a little bit of an ass, and I expect to get talked to a certain way, but Owens didn't deserve that. So, I swivel my stool around and make sure to make eye contact with crazy tits.

"I strongly advise that you not talk to my assistant like that ever again," I warn.

"Are you threatening me?" Her voice rises to a shrill decibel.

I stand up, but not to threaten, but because I'm aware of how my large size can defuse many escalating situations. It shuts them down. And usually I don't have to say a word. Crazy tits keeps her eyes on me but takes a small step back.

Owens awkwardly places her body directly in front of mine, losing her balance for a moment, so I catch her. For the few moments that I hold her, I can feel that her body is tense. Uncomfortable with my discovery, she quickly steps outside of my embrace.

"I apologize for any misunderstanding. No one is threatening anyone. I just wanted to thank you and your mother for your service today, Miss ... same last name as Stephanie's?"

"No, my mom remarried. I'm a McCoy."

"Thank you, Miss McCoy."

The woman's tight grip around her instrument of destruction loosens a bit, but now she's pointing it at me while still speaking to Owens.

"Do you actually work for this bully?" she asks as if just the notion of working for me is repugnant. The nerve of this gold digger.

I start to respond to her totally unfair and inaccurate description of me with some caustic words of my own when Owens discreetly jabs me in the abdomen again. So I stay quiet.

"Yes, I do."

"Then I feel sorry as hell for you."

Owens body finally relaxes as she sighs.

"You're not the only one who does."

CHAPTER EIGHT

COOP

Are you fucking kidding me?

I'm not sure if everyone suddenly woke up and bumped their heads on their nightstands this morning, but all of a sudden, I'm the bad guy?

The ill-mannered, underdressed caterer gives me the stink eye as she walks back over to the craft services table, and my seriously late assistant decides to lay into me.

"I leave you on your own for one hour and this is the trouble you get yourself into?"

"Ninety minutes, and it was *that* woman who was nothing but trouble."

"That's not how it looked to me."

"You always blame me."

"Who else is there to blame?"

"Have you been working for me for the last three years or am I talking to your doppelgänger? You know the deal. These women are crazy nowadays. Did you see her shirt?"

"Did I see that her nipples were showing, *mawmaw*? Why yes, I did. So what? You've never seen nipples before? Is the big bad football star unable to control himself if someone shows him a little nip?"

"That's how you talk to your boss when you're," I tap the face of my Rolex, "ninety minutes late?"

"Free the nip!" she cheers like the goofball she is.

"All this fervor about nipples from the most conservative woman I've ever met."

"I'm not conservative, I'm professional. There's a difference."

"You work for a football player, not the CEO of some bank."

"You're more than a football player."

"Why thank you," I say in a playful manner. "I'm very much aware that I'm so much more."

She rolls her eyes.

"You know what I mean."

"Yes, I know. Beyond being ridiculously talented

on the football field, I am also an entrepreneurial juggernaut. I even amaze myself sometimes."

"Whatever," she mutters. "Listen, you didn't have to be so rude to the woman. One more word out of you and she would have sued you for sexual harassment or assault."

"I didn't touch her. I barely looked at her."

"She's probably talking crap about you on Twitter as we speak, and we certainly don't need that headache. I've worked hard to keep your social media squeaky clean after the last stunt you pulled."

"The last stunt? You mean the stripper?"

"Oh, I forgot about that one."

"I didn't even talk to that woman."

"Are you sure? You were drunk."

Her judgmental tone rubs me the wrong way, but I can't deny that Owens is right. I've caused a few drunken scenes in my past. Made a few mistakes. Made a lot of enemies. And Owens makes it all go away. She can work miracles.

"Yeah but that catering woman with the fat nipples was already building the in-ground pool."

"Building the what?"

"You know the type of women I'm talking about. In her mind she was already building our ten thousand square foot home and planning the pool I was going to have to pay for once she trapped me with a baby."

"Wowza, Coop! You have some serious trust issues."

Owens is such a nerd. It's cute. Who the hell says wowza?

"For good reason."

"You think every woman wants to trap you."

"I'm a fucking catch."

"And that every man wants to be you."

"That's just basic facts."

"Alternative facts," she mutters under her breath.

"I heard that."

"Let's just go over today's schedule."

I'm not letting her off of the hook that easy.

"Before discussing my schedule, why don't you tell me why you're so late today? All of this could have been avoided if you had been here on time doing your job. I pay you to keep the vultures away."

"You also pay me to do a million other things. I'm only one person, and I was working on the arrangements for the school's open house extravaganza."

"You use the strangest words."

"What's strange about extravaganza?"

"It's an open house for parents. You're overstating things by calling it an extravaganza."

She looks offended.

"Educated people say extravaganza."

"Educated people say wowza too?"

"Yes!" she exclaims angrily.

"Educated weirdos."

"Do you want to go over your schedule or not?"

"I do but after you tell me what you were specifically working on that made you ninety minutes late."

"I had to meet with the principal to talk about who is on deck to speak that night. There's going to be press coverage for the ribbon cutting ceremony, and I needed to make sure it's going to be right."

"You will be there to make sure it's right."

"I'd rather be anal about things now instead of having to troubleshoot things later."

"Damn, Owens, you're pulling out all the stops for my kids," I say after considering all the time she's spent working on the open house so far and her attention to detail. "If I had known you'd be this invested in it, I would have built a school sooner."

"You're doing a good thing, Coop. I just want to make sure it gets the attention it deserves."

She doesn't look at me directly in the eyes when she says that which is strange. Owens always looks me dead in the eyes when she talks to me, especially when it's about business. That's part of the reason why I trust her to plan my entire life. She's not intimidated by me and will always give it to me straight. I can depend on her. I can trust her.

"Well it's just one open house," I say. Shaking off the odd vibes she's giving me. "There will be others. Don't let that one day interfere with your main responsibilities again. Part of which is to cock block all gold diggers. If that woman would have had it her way, she would have left the set today pregnant with my love child."

"Lucky for her." Owens grins. "I just saved her from a lifetime of being forever stuck with you."

"Go get me some more pie before I fire you," I quip.

"Would you? Could you? Pretty please?" She presses her palms into a prayer formation as if she's begging me to fire her.

I can't help but laugh to myself. When Owens first came to be my assistant, she was a walking disaster. She was quiet, timid, unorganized, and unconfident. I was tough on her at first because I knew that everyone in my world would be ten times tougher on her. Through trial and error, and a bit of tough love, slowly she began to learn. Now she's a hard worker, fearless in negotiation, and she can totally hold her own with anyone who comes before her—including me.

She's so spoiled.

"As if you'd *ever* leave me."

CHAPTER NINE

URSULA

I'm not a huge coffee drinker, but not everyone can say that they receive free coffee for life from Dunkin' Donuts (one of the perks of my job), so today I'm ordering a medium sized vanilla iced coffee. To heck with the calories. I'm celebrating. Today, I'm finally going to say what I need to say to Coop. The awards are over. The open house plans are tight. It's time to tell him.

It's the fifth of the month and this is the day Coop sets aside, when his schedule permits, to stop by his Dunkin' Donuts franchise near Coney Island in Brooklyn. He discreetly looks around, takes pics with fans if they recognize him, and then briefly goes over the sales figures with the manager. It's my job to examine the cleanliness of the counter area, the back office, and to check in with employees.

When he first opened the franchise, the area was in a time of heavy transition. Not a lot of developers could see the vision or wanted to take the risk investing in the decaying neighborhood, but Coop could see the potential. Now he owns a good chunk of prime property along the city's revitalized ocean front area.

"How are things here?" I ask one of my favorite shift supervisors. She's a young, single mother who seems to love it here. "I think you were having trouble with that one girl on the evening shift."

"That girl is still a raging bitch, but thankfully I don't see her much. I work days, and Bobby puts her on nights."

"I'm not sure that's a permanent solution though."

"Why not?"

"Well if you want to be considered for management at some point, you're going to have to learn how to deal with difficult personalities."

"Mmm, I guess that's true but—"

"I'm telling you this, because I want to see you succeed."

"I know but—"

"You have to imagine what that girl's worst case

scenario could be. What could she be working through in her life? Now imagine she has to deal with all of that and still come to work every day."

"I didn't think of it that way."

"We all have our burdens to bear right?"

"I guess so. I'm not sure what yours would be, but I guess so."

"Trust me. I have my issues too. We all do."

"So basically, you're saying be flexible."

"Exactly ... if Bobby has to continually consider your issues when he's making the work schedule for the week, is he likely to recommend you for the next management spot?"

"Wow, I definitely didn't think about it like that. I'm so glad Mr. Barnes asks you to check in with us. You're awesome, Ursula. You see things in a way that I would have never considered."

"You're so welcome. I only want to help."

"Extra whipped cream for you today, girl."

"Whoop! Whoop!"

Since Coop gave Tito the day off, after we're finished at the store, we jump in an Uber to head to Coop's office building in Manhattan near the entrance to the Brooklyn Bridge. I decide that this is the perfect opportunity to tell him.

"The store looked really good didn't it?"

"Yep, everything looked great. I'm pleased with the progress. Are the employees okay? I saw you talking a long time to Diane."

"They're fine. Just giving her some tips."

"Oh, okay. She seems smart."

"Yeah, she is. I like her a lot for the next management position that comes up."

Coop owns four Dunkin' Donut franchises.

"Whatever you think is fine. When the time comes, you can make it happen."

Ugh, I think to myself. I won't be around to make it happen.

"Should I make reservations for you and Kiera tonight?" I ask in an attempt to stall a bit longer.

Kiera is Coop's newest fling. She's basically just another Megan. Her claim to fame is that she's slept with enough famous men to become relevant. I don't understand it. Honestly, I think that Coop is a huge hypocrite.

He thinks that every woman but his mother is out to get him for his wealth, yet he brings home these trashy women who make a living sleeping around or posing half-naked for money? I called him on it once and his explanation to me was that *at least women like Megan and Kiera are upfront about what they want. They want money, they want fame, and they want to* be seen. In return, they give him plenty of no-strings-attached sex. Every man's dream.

"No, I want to go over some of the school applications again. I'll see her later."

Coop is very much involved with the opening of the school. It's a college preparatory high school specifically for boys who live in Brooklyn and are from underprivileged backgrounds. They will receive a free education, free computers, free uniforms, free breakfast and lunch, and handholding through their college process. It's a huge undertaking and clearly something he's passionate about, which is why he likes to be involved with the application process.

"I presorted them for you using the applicant's previous middle school and current GPA. They're on your desk."

Coop looks up from his phone.

"Thanks, Owens. Have I told you lately how awesome you are?"

"Uh, no. I'm not sure that you have ever told me how awesome I am."

"Stop playing. I'm sure I have at some point."

He continues working on his phone.

Uh, no you never have.

"So ... listen ... I wanted to talk to you about something."

I rub my palms nervously against my thighs.

"Yep," he answers curtly. Still obviously distracted by his phone. "What is it?"

"Have you ever considered getting a new assistant?"

Coop sits his phone down, pivots his entire body, and stares at me straight on.

"What?"

"A new assistant."

"What would I need a new assistant for? I have you."

"Yeah, that's the thing."

I look down at my hands and start twisting my emerald ring around. It was my mother's and has always been my good luck charm.

"Look at me, Owens."

I clench my hands and look my employer in the eyes. I don't know why I'm so nervous. I was so sure about my decision. I've been sure about it for months now. I'm an actress, not an assistant, and I need to finally go and actually *be* an actress.

"I'm quitting, Coop."

"You're quitting?"

"Yes."

"You are quitting?"

"Yes."

"What are you going to do if you don't work for me?"

"I don't know yet."

"You don't know? What the hell kind of answer is that?"

"An honest one."

"Who's trying to poach you? Stevenson? Johnson? One of the agencies?"

"No, Coop. No one is trying to hire me from under you. This is all my decision."

He stares at me with what I think is a look of pure confusion. I think he's about to say something to me, but then he stops himself.

"I've been thinking about this for a while now but don't worry. I'm not going to leave you high and dry. I'm going to help hire my replacement."

"You're making a mistake, Owens."

"This doesn't mean that I'm ungrateful. I realize what an opportunity this has been, and I thank you for it, but it's time for me to move on."

"If that's what you want to do—"

He bends his head back down and begins typing furiously on his phone.

I find his reaction a bit surprising, but I won't let it unnerve me.

The hard part is over.

"Thank you for everything."

"You said that already."

We arrive to our destination in total silence. Coop gets out of the car and starts walking with large strides inside of the building. It's not that he doesn't normally walk in front of me, he can't help to with his colossal frame and long legs, but this time I can tell it's purposeful.

He can't get away from me fast enough.

CHAPTER TEN

COOP

I tried to drink it away—I've reached my limit.

Sex it away—Not in the mood. Not even to masturbate.

And now I've tried sleeping it away—But that shit's not working either.

I've been in bed lying in a supine position, with my hands behind my head, for exactly thirty-five minutes and have come to the conclusion that I will never sleep again. Not until I understand why Owens would want to resign.

It makes zero sense.

She's got to be fucking with my head.

I'm the perfect boss to work for. We get along. I

pay her well. She's a natural as my second-in-command. What else could her ungrateful ass want?

Dammit! I'm out of vodka and Tylenol PM. I need sleep. I need some clarity. I'm going to call her. It's the only thing left to do. She answers on the third ring.

"Coop?"

"Were you sleeping?"

It's obvious she was in a deep sleep. Damn deserter. Probably dreaming about whatever the hell girls like Owens dream about. Puppies, rappers, Louis Vuitton bags. Hell, if I know. I'm just glad I woke her ass up. How dare she sleep like a baby after the bomb she just dropped on me.

"Everyone living in the Eastern Standard Time zone is sleeping. It's almost three a.m."

"I just want to be clear."

"About?"

"Your announcement comes at a very inconvenient time for me."

"When would have been a better time to announce that I'm moving on?"

"Don't be a smart-ass, Owens. It doesn't become you."

Actually, she's always been a smart-ass. It's one of the things I find most endearing about her.

"Say what you called to say, Mr. Barnes."

"Oh, it's Mr. Barnes now?"

"It probably should have always been Mr. Barnes. We've totally been way too casual with each other."

Is that why she's leaving? She wants me to be a dickhead boss? What a masochist.

"Then I'll keep things *not so casual* with you. You can't just leave. I've given you way too much responsibility. So, you've got thirty days to hire and train a suitable replacement. I have too many good things going on in my life right now for a change in assistants to mess it up. I want a smooth transition. It's the least that you owe me for giving you such an amazing opportunity."

Soft snoring.

"OWENS!"

"I heard you," she says sleepily. "Thirty days. Replacement. I'm on it."

I end the call abruptly.

Pissed more than ever.

Bright-eyed and bushy-tailed.

I make another call.

"Hello?"

My friend and teammate Saint answers the phone with a gravelly voice. I realize it's three in the morning, but if I can't get a decent night's sleep then neither should my quarterback.

"Hey."

"Coop?"

"Yeah, it's me."

"Are you in jail?"

"No."

"The hospital?"

"Nope."

"Then, dude, I'm going to kick your ass at training tomorrow. It's three fucking a.m. What the hell do you want?"

"Sleep eludes me."

"What?"

"I can't sleep."

"And that's my problem because?"

"Owens asked to resign or rather she told me she was resigning."

Saint's phone starts to make rustling sounds. I think I hear his wife Sabrina cursing me out in the background. He tells her that it's me on the phone and that she should go back to sleep. I should feel guilty that I've woken her up too, but I don't. I've decided it's all Owens' fault. She's to blame.

"You called me at this time of night to discuss employee problems?"

"Yes."

"You're upset that she quit?"

"Fuck yeah. I'm pissed."

"Did you think she was going to stay with you indefinitely? You probably suck to work for."

"It's only been three years not thirty! I'm in the middle of some of the most important work in my life right now. I'm at the prime of my career. I'm opening the school. I'm thinking of buying some other properties. She can't leave. She picked the worst time to decide to leave."

"So you hire someone else, Coop. Ursula is not the only capable assistant out there."

"She's the only assistant!"

Saint is quiet for a moment.

"Dude, you're losing it."

"I'm tired as fuck. Sorry."

"Are you sure this isn't about something else?"

"Such as?"

I get up and put on a baseball cap. Then I slide my cell phone inside of it next to my ear, so I won't have to hold it. I start scouring the kitchen for something half decent to eat and end up slamming the refrigerator closed. All I have is healthy shit in here. No white sugar, no white flour my ass. I want Oreos.

"Do you have feelings for her?"

"Have you been hit in the head too many times?"

"Have you? You're the one calling me in the middle of the night over some girl."

"You call her *some girl* again and—"

Saints starts laughing hysterically.

"You'll what, Coop? You gonna kick my ass over *some girl?*"

I'm going to throttle him tomorrow.

"I should have known better than to call you about this."

"And why is that?"

He's practically snorting laughter through the phone at this point.

"Sabrina keeps your life in order. You've never needed an assistant like I do."

"I keep my own life in order."

"The hell you do."

"Hire someone else, Coop. That's all I can tell you."

That's not going to help me get to sleep tonight.

"Forget I called. You wouldn't understand."

"Oh, I understand what you need all right." He continues with his incessant laughing. "I'm going to tell coach to give you the concussion protocol tomorrow. I think you have one. What's ironic about this is that you're filthy rich, marginally attractive—"

"Hey!"

"And so thick headed that you don't realize what's going on. You want Owens to sit on your face. End of story. That shit is funny."

"Saint, I swear to fucking God!"

I want to reach through the phone and strangle him. My supposed friend. The only person besides Tito I tell anything to, and look what it gets me. The jackass is laughing so hard that the phone drops, and Sabrina ends up picking it up.

"Coop," she says sternly.

"Hi, Sabrina, I—"

"Stop talking."

"But—"

"Whatever you're saying has triggered my husband into a fit of laughter and literally ten seconds away from peeing in our bed."

"But I needed to talk and—"

"Stop."

I shut my mouth.

"Peeing in my bed is not an option. So, I highly recommend that you talk about whatever this is tomorrow, because if I don't get back to sleep in the next ten minutes, I could easily miscalculate someone's payroll tomorrow."

I contract Sabrina's business management firm to manage employee payroll and taxes for all of my businesses. It's probably not a good idea to get on her bad side. I didn't think this through.

"I'll talk to him later. Sorry, Sabrina."

"Wise decision."

"Think about it, Coop!" I hear Saint yell and then a rustling sound in the background. *Are the two of them actually wrestling for the phone?* "Think about why you can't sleep. She's not just your employee, dummy. She's a whole lot more."

Sabrina lets out what sounds like a yelp laced with pleasure and then the phone goes dead.

I guess payroll is going to be late anyway.

URSULA

I pop my earbuds in and sift through my small cooler of goodies, pulling out an ice-cold Fiji Water and laying it on the back of my neck. It's hot as hades outside, and I'm sitting on a scorching university bleacher at Nighthawks training camp, watching half-clothed men run plays, while I listen to the soundtrack of *Mamma Mia*.

There are sixteen training camp practices open to the public during the season. Fifteen are during the day and one is at night. Until my last day working for Coop, part of my job still includes attending them, because press is always here, and Coop doesn't talk to the press. He says it's a distraction, but it's probably more like a phobia. A normal, arrogant, alpha ball player loves to talk about themselves to anyone who will listen. They love an audience. Not Coop.

"Hi, gorgeous."

I pull my left earbud out.

"Hey, Jim."

Jim McKinney is a local sports reporter in the city. He can't be too much older than me, but he has made himself well known among the seasoned press pit reporters already. He's extremely ambitious and persistent. I can always depend on him to ask me two things whenever I see him: for an opportunity at an exclusive interview with Coop and for a date.

"I see your guy is looking pretty good this year. Did he drop a couple of pounds?"

"I wouldn't know. He looks the same to me."

I crack open and chug down half of my bottled water while I watch Coop and Saint Stevenson run a few plays together. They both look a little tired today.

"How's his hearing this season?"

"Same as it's always been."

Coop has partial hearing loss in his left ear. It's the result of some sort of non-football related injury that happened when he was young. A time in his life that he prefers not to talk about. Unfortunately, journalists have reported lots of wild theories about how the hearing loss happened which is another reason why Coop won't talk to them. One time a reporter wrote that the injury was due to an altercation between Coop and his dad when he was a kid. A total lie, which Coop's dad had to deny for years—he's a college football coach—and for which Coop has never forgiven the reporters.

"What does he think about the new guys on the team? They gave up a lot to acquire Parinzino. Is he meshing well with the other players?"

"Aren't these questions for the coaching staff?"

"I think you would know better than any of the coaches."

"That's where you're wrong."

"Nah, I think you're holding out on me, Ursula, in more ways than one."

He licks the corner of his lips, and I almost throw up a little in my mouth.

"I'll give you one thing, Jim, you're definitely persistent."

"What?" He feigns innocence.

"You know I'm not going to reveal anything that Coop tells me, and to be honest with you, we don't talk about what's said in the locker room. It's like Vegas in there. Whatever goes on in there stays in there."

"I guess that makes sense, because football isn't

really his major priority anyway, right? You think he'll retire soon?"

This is another running storyline that the press has continually tried to shove down fans' throats as if it's a fact when it isn't. The media assumes that because football isn't Coop's primary source of income that it must not be as important to him as it is to other players. How soon they forget that football was first.

Coop comes from hard working people in Georgia that live, eat, poop, and breathe football. Nothing was handed to him. All the success he has built has come as a direct result of hard work and the wealth he first accumulated as a football player.

It's a shame how if he makes one mistake on the field they blame it on the "distractions" in his life aka his empire: Dunkin' Donut franchises, pizza shops, tattoo shops, movie theaters, and soon his new high school for boys.

While I know that their assumptions about Coop are unfair and untrue, I guess it doesn't help that he acts so standoffish with reporters. Maybe they would find something else to write about if he would talk to them about something. Of course, that's going to be the new assistant's problem to manage now. Not mine.

"Now you know that isn't true, Jim."

"How would I know what's true or what isn't when he doesn't ever talk to us?"

I shrug my shoulders like I have a million times before.

"I can't control who Coop talks to."

"He's contractually obligated to talk to the press. He knows that, right?"

"Take it up with the NFL then."

"Oh, come on, Ursula, it would be great publicity for him. I'll even let him cherry pick his questions."

"The answer is the same ... I can't help."

A few of the reporters sitting in front of us start laughing. They're old-timers who have been working the Nighthawk beat for over twenty years.

"You two sound like last season," one of them says.

"Same song different summer," the other chimes in.

I stick my earbuds back in and hum along to ABBA while I check on some of the applications the head-hunting agency sent over. Now that I've finally told Coop that I'm leaving I feel like a huge weight has been lifted. I notice one application that shines a little more than the rest. I'm going to call her for an initial interview and get this ball rolling. If I like her, I'll bring her in to meet Coop.

"So, what about dinner then?"

I try to act like I don't hear Jim's question, but he taps me on the knee to make sure that he gets my attention. Like I said, the guy is persistent.

"Oh, I'm sorry. I was listening to music. Did you say something?"

"I asked if you wanted to grab dinner tonight."

I've never been comfortable turning a man down, probably because I don't have a whole lot of experience at it. I haven't dated much at all really. It's not that I didn't want to, but I either didn't have the time or didn't like who was doing the asking. This time my reasoning leans toward the latter. Jim is probably a good guy, but he's just not my type.

"Oh sorry, I can't. I have to work."

"She only has time to deal with one big personality at a time, McKinney. Barnes is all she can handle," says one of the old cronies up front. The two of them get on my nerves sometimes. They're like those two old guys from the Muppets. They think they can say anything they want and that no one is going to check them because they're old. The most annoying thing about it is that for the most part they're right.

"Speaking of big personalities, here comes Coop now."

I can hear the collective sigh of every woman on the bleachers.

He's shirtless.

Dripping in perspiration.

Covered in tats.

And approaching us with a ball in his hand and a mischievous grin across his face.

CHAPTER TWELVE

URSULA

"Ahhhh!"

I release a blood curdling scream that comes from deep within my chest. Coop just shook his hair out like he's some sort of soaking wet Labrador Retriever, and sweat just flew all over me and probably ten other people too. I'm not a big fan of sweat, especially when it belongs to someone else.

I quickly react and stand up, sticking my arms straight out away from my body in revulsion. My cell phone and ear buds drop like a rock through the slats of the bleachers. One entire side of the field turns to see where the death cry originated from. Most of them wearing a momentary look of concern on their faces until they see where and particularly who it's coming from.

Me.

"Oh, it's just Coop," someone says casually from the sidelines. "He's hysterical."

They comment as if it's a usual occurrence to see Coop terrorizing me like some sort of fraternity boy hazing a neophyte. Uh, reality check people. This isn't normal.

Coop and I haven't said much to each other since last night, but it's obvious that he's not pleased with me. I didn't think he would be, but I guess he's pissed that I quit, and he didn't see it coming, and probably that I fell asleep on the phone last night too. It explains the sweat bath. This is how he expresses himself when he's fuming. Like a thirteen-year-old brat.

I can feel the muscles in my neck tighten when Coop lets out a deep boisterous laugh at my expense and tosses me a damp towel with the Nighthawks logo on it.

"Here, Owens. Don't ever say I never gave you anything."

I almost use the thing to wipe myself off when it dawns on me that it's damp because it's also soaked with Coop's sweat, so I throw it right back at him, which only encourages him to laugh even harder.

"No thanks. You looked a little tired out there today. You probably need it more."

I use my next best option and turn my T-shirt up to wipe my face forgetting for a moment that I don't wear a bra most days in the summer. Luckily before I flash anyone my teacup sized boobs, Coop throws the balled-up towel back hard at me. It hits me with a thump in the center in my chest.

"Ouch!"

"Stop flashing your boobs to the fans," he says gruffly. "You'll frighten the children."

I allow my shirt to fall down as the spectators around us including the same two grumpy grandpas up front try badly to hold back their laughter. I've long since decided that most people here today are drunk. Four or five beers, drinking in this heat, and everything starts to seem a little funny.

"Excuse me. We don't mean to interrupt, but do you mind signing an autograph for my boy, Mr. Barnes?"

A woman with a kind face, who's been sitting within earshot of us, asks Coop for an autograph for her son who is standing quietly by her side. While Coop chooses to avoid the media, he acts much differently with his fans. I wipe my hands off on my leggings and pull a promotional picture out of my bag and hand it to him along with a Sharpie.

"What's your name?" He crouches down to ask the boy.

"Craig."

"Nice to meet you, Craig. Do you play football?"

"Yes, sir."

"What position do you play?"

"Coach said I'm small, so they made me a free safety."

"Awesome. That's a great position. That means you're fast."

The little boy's eyes light up from the compliment.

"Did you have a good time today?"

"Yup!"

"You weren't bored?"

"No, sir. Not even a little bit."

"Are the Nighthawks your favorite team?"

"Yes, sir."

"Who's your favorite player on the team?"

The boy presses his lips together and leans in closer to his mom. It's cute that he's reluctant to speak, because it's obvious that his favorite player isn't Coop. He's wearing Saint's jersey.

"It's all right if it isn't me." Coop pats his shoulder. "I can take it."

"Mr. Barnes asked you a question, Craig." His mother encourages him to answer.

"Well … I really like you a lot."

"Uh-huh and?"

"But my favorite player is Saint Stevenson."

"Yeah?"

"Is that okay?"

"Definitely. Because guess what? Saint is one of my favorite players too."

A look of relief washes over the boy's face that makes me believe there is hope yet for my employer. In this moment, I can see a glimpse of the man Coop can be: sweet, kind, warm and compassionate.

"Really?"

"Best quarterback in the league." Coop signs and hands back the photo and a football that the boy was holding. "Here you go."

"What do you say, sweetie?" his mother asks.

"Thank you, Mr. Barnes."

"You're welcome."

It's inevitable that when Coop signs one autograph a line starts. I've come prepared with plenty of photos and Sharpies, and we whiz through the line like a well oiled machine. After we're finished, Coop jogs around the side and under the bleachers to retrieve my phone.

"Listen, I'm done for the day," he says as he wipes

off my phone screen on his shorts. "Gonna hit the showers and then I'm going to need Tito to bring the car around here in thirty."

"I'm the one who needs a *bloody* shower."

"Have you been watching that British version of *American Idol* again?" he asks while handing me my phone back.

It's irritating that he knows me so well. I have a bad habit of picking up accents or the colloquialisms of people on shows that I binge watch. It must be the actress in me.

"Sugar, honey, iced tea—the screen is cracked!" I stare at my phone in horror. "I can't text Tito. You're going to have to do it."

My whole life is on my phone, and as a matter of fact, Coop's whole life is on it too.

"Did you just spell out the word shit?" he asks mid chuckle. "Sugar, *honey*, *i*ced tea?"

"I don't use profanity in the workplace," I say. "Something you should consider."

"Where'd you hear that saying? You even used a bad southern accent when you said it."

"My accent isn't bad, and it's an old saying."

"Yeah, but you must have heard it recently."

I suck my teeth.

He really does know me too well.

"On a reality show, but never mind about that, because the more important issue right now is that my phone looks like Charlotte's Web and I won't be able to get any work done."

The cracks in the screen have formed what looks like an intricate spider web.

"You can't make it work for the next thirty days?"

He uses a sarcastic tone.

"Very funny."

"I'm not laughing."

"Me either. Your life over the next thirty days is in this phone."

"I'm sure you synced it to a calendar on your laptop."

"Seriously!? I need my phone. I can't carry around my laptop everywhere."

"All right, already, I'll get you a new one," he says dismissively. "It's insured."

"Dang nabbit, I can't open the calendar." I try pressing the home button several times. "I can't open any apps."

I know that I must sound like a crazy person.

"I *said* I'll get you a new one," he repeats more emphatically as he jogs toward the locker rooms. "Stop spazzing the fuck out. And don't say dang nabbit ever again."

"I want it today!" I holler back.

He throws up a thumbs-up signal and continues his retreat.

"And a case!"

He throws up another okay sign.

"Hey, Coop!" Jim calls out after him. "You ready to give me that exclusive yet?"

Coop stops dead in his tracks in the middle of the field with his back still to us.

"What are you doing?" I angrily whisper to Jim.

"Something my father taught me to do—just ask."

URSULA

"You wait until he's halfway to the locker room to ask him for an interview?"

Coop turns around and cocks his head to one side. He starts walking in long, purposeful steps back toward where I'm seated.

"That was not the right way to ask him," I say through gritted teeth.

I don't need any drama these next thirty days. It will take me months to change the narrative in the news if Coop ends up threatening Jim.

"Don't worry, Urs." Jim pats my arm in a patronizing manner. "I got this."

"Who are you?" Coop demands to know as he approaches Jim.

Everyone is staring at us. I see a few spectator phones in the air.

"They're taping us," I whisper to Coop.

He throws his hand up to silence me.

"Name?" he asks Jim again.

"Jim McKinney. Daily Examiner."

Jim holds out his hand for a handshake. Coop doesn't reciprocate the gesture. He just gives Jim a cursory glance and then turns to me.

"Is he a friend of yours, Owens?"

"He's been on the beat for two years, Coop," I answer defensively because I feel like he's accusing me of something.

Even if he doesn't talk to reporters, Coop should know who works the Nighthawk beat. He sees them all season and Jim writes about him specifically practically every Sunday. It's not like I put him up to this.

"That isn't what I asked you."

"Yes, he's a friend."

Friend is a bit of an exaggeration.

"So, you want me to be nice? You want me to be *professional* with him?"

That was clearly a jab in reference to our conversation yesterday. I swear I can hear Carla and Monica's voices in my head. What was I thinking? I didn't realize he would react so badly to this. I should have given him more of a warning.

"Yes, that would be awesome," I say through a forced smile.

He turns to Jim.

"Okay, Jim McKinney, on the strength of Owens here I'll give you thirty minutes on a day and time of my choosing. She'll arrange it."

Every reporter in close proximity turns their heads with their mouths wide opened. Some are shocked, some are aghast, and some are pissed. I certainly don't blame them. There are veteran reporters here who haven't been able to get a peep out of Coop since he joined the team. He's only doing this to prove some sort of convoluted point.

"Thanks so much!"

"You're welcome and McKinney—"

"Yes?"

"The name is Mr. Barnes not Coop."

"Oh, I apologize ... Mr. Barnes."

"It's not that I mind so much, but our girl Owens here doesn't like casual. It makes her ... uncomfortable."

Jim looks quizzically at me.

I think the reporter in him senses more is going on than meets the eye.

"I'll text Tito myself, Owens. Meet me in the parking lot in thirty."

I don't respond but instead sit back down, place my damaged phone on the bleachers, and reach in my cooler for my turkey wrap. I'm famished. Being on the receiving end of Cooper Barnes's wrath is taxing to say the least. This is going to be a long effin' thirty days.

"What gives?" One of the old cronies turns and asks. "Seriously, Ursula, we've been wanting that interview for years. We're the veteran reporters here. What the hell was that?"

I can't respond because my mouth is full of a big bite of turkey.

"That was me getting the interview that you guys were too chickenshit to ask for over the last five years," Jim croons.

"Fuck you."

The mom who asked for the autograph covers her boy's ears.

"Watch your mouths," I reprimand them all like I'm their mother.

Jim touches my arm.

"I owe you big time for this one, Ursula. That interview may help me get a regular column. You have to let me buy you dinner. As a thank you ... nothing more. You know unless you say differently."

I stare contemplatively at my bland pita wrap. The processed turkey. The fake American cheese. A metaphor for my life so far.

Mediocrity.

I've taken the first step and quit my job. I know Jim's dinner invitation probably means more to him than a thank you, but maybe now it's time for me to take a second step outside of my normal box.

What could it hurt?

"Okay, Jim. One dinner."

URSULA

"I need to talk to you."

"Hi, I'm fine. How are you?"

"I don't have time for pleasantries."

"What is it, Monica?"

"I did your chart last night, and the stars are clear, this isn't a good time to make a life changing decision. Your moon is in Sagittarius. Did you quit yet?"

"You do realize that astrology isn't real, right?"

"Tell a billion Chinese people that shit."

"They don't believe in it either, Monica. You're a nut job."

"And I guess you don't believe in global warming either?"

"Yes, I believe in global warming, but the two of them are not even remotely related. One is based in science fiction and the other in actual science."

"Says you. Anyway, I'm telling you it clearly says in your chart to wait before making any big career decisions. It won't hurt for you to just hold off a minute and go on your passion seeking mission when the stars are better aligned."

"It's too late for all of that."

"You did it?"

"It's done."

"And? What did he say? I'm putting Carla on a conference call with us."

"Don't do that, I have a meeting in a little while. She'll want to stay on the phone half of the afternoon."

"Okay, spill the tea to me then. I'll recap for her later."

"There's no tea. He had a little bit of an attitude, but for the most part it went well like I thought it would." Not exactly true. "He wants to make sure that I find a replacement and train him or her before I leave, which I agreed was totally fair. So that's what I'm in the middle of handling today."

"Wow, I didn't think he'd be so agreeable."

"I told you so. Maybe your charts aren't always accurate."

"Yeah, that's the thing. The charts are usually pretty precise. So, you definitely told him you're leaving and that was it? He just said 'okay find me a new girl'?"

"Well ... he did end up calling me in the middle of the night to talk about it again."

"Uh-huh, now we're getting somewhere."

"I guess that I did take him by surprise. It's not like I gave any prior indication that I wanted to leave, so he was just looking for more of an explanation. You know probably wanting to make sure that it wasn't anything he did."

"Well it was something he did, right? You're leaving because he's such a horrible boss."

"I never said he was horrible."

"That's funny because that seems like all you've ever said about him. You had no life. We don't know him. He's not what we think—"

I stop her there.

"You misinterpreted. This is about me not him. I just want a change. I'm an actress, so I should be on television, right? Putting the degree that the good folks of First Methodist Church paid for to use."

"Have you started lining up auditions then?"

"Not yet. I have to give Coop his thirty days, train

the new assistant, and then I can focus my energies elsewhere."

"So where are you headed now?"

"The office. The applicant I selected is coming in to meet him."

"A woman?"

"Yes."

"Did you tell her anything about him?"

"Due to a confidentiality clause, the agency doesn't reveal who the client is until the last minute. It's to protect the client's privacy. She doesn't know that it's Coop yet."

"Well were you at least able to warn her of the type of commitment the job requires?"

"Absolutely not. I want her to take the job, don't I?"

Due to Coop's hectic schedule we don't usually spend a large amount of time in the office, which is probably a good thing because he only rents one floor of the building that we're in. While the space includes his office suite, my office, a large conference room, a weight room, a kitchenette, and a multipurpose area where Tito spends much of his time catching up on sports; it's small enough that it makes it difficult to avoid each other. But today, I have no choice but to deal with him.

I knock on his office door and promptly enter the room. I watch him for a moment. He's on the floor, shirtless, in loose sweatpants doing his daily set of push-ups. He always has his shirt off, but lately it's distracting.

"What are you doing?"

"My workout. What does it look like?"

"I told you I have an applicant coming in. A good one."

"So, bring her in."

"I thought we were keeping things professional."

"I can't wear sweats?"

"For someone that hates the attention of random women so much, you sure seem to have your shirt off all the time."

He lifts his head and stares at me while continuing his workout. I can't help but notice the definition of each of his muscles in his upper body as he effortlessly powers through the set.

"That doesn't give your gender the right to ogle me." He grins mischievously.

Get it together, Ursula.

"You're about to conduct an interview. Put a shirt on."

"I'm a football player. I always have my shirt off. If she can't handle a little skin, then this isn't the job for her. And remember, if you can't find someone to take over for you then you can't leave. That's in your contract, *Miss Owens*."

"I don't remember reading that."

"That's because you had a shitty lawyer. I remember her. She was sliding me her number on a business card during your contract review. Big thighs. Soft mouth."

"That's a lie! She wasn't flirting with you."

"Actually, she was. I definitely hit that."

"You're disgusting."

Coop finishes his set of push-ups, stands up, then watches me closely as I reluctantly follow the line of sweat that drips from his throat down to the V of his abdomen.

"I thought you didn't like sweat?" he asks with a smug look on his face.

"I'm gagging as we speak."

His voice deepens. "Does it make you angry that I slept with your lawyer?"

"That woman is from my church," I snarl.

"Praise the Lord."

"I'll buzz you when my replacement gets here. It can't be soon enough for me."

I storm out in a blaze. Tito doesn't say anything when I whiz by him in the common area without saying hello. I already know what he's thinking. It's written all over his face.

Since when have I cared who Cooper Barnes sleeps with?

CHAPTER FIFTEEN

URSULA

The man at the front desk of the building lets me know once my applicant has arrived, so I go downstairs to meet her in the lobby. Her name is Jane Perez, and she looks exactly as I desperately hoped she wouldn't. She's freakin' gorgeous.

A beautiful woman with honey colored skin and plenty of brunette hair that hangs in soft waves to her bra line. She has an hourglass figure, a gentle smile, and I stare at her with envy for a moment because her breasts are definitely not like my teacups—they're jugs.

I should have hired a man.

"Miss Perez?"

"Hi, Miss Owens. It's such a pleasure to finally meet you."

We shake hands and I can't even find fault in that either. Her hand is warm but not clammy, slender but not fragile, and her nails are painted the perfect nude tone. I'm lucky if I can fit in a manicure on the holidays.

"Thank you for coming in. I've reviewed your qualifications and checked your references and I think that you may be a good match, but obviously the final decision comes down to my boss. We'll go straight up to meet him unless you have any questions for me."

One of the great things about the head-hunting agency we use is that they fill positions for high profile employers anonymously. The applicants don't get to know who's doing the hiring until they come for the final interview which is exactly what we're doing today.

The big reveal.

"Umm, no questions."

Hmm, maybe Jane's one flaw is finally exposed. Now that we're on our way to meet Coop, she's turned a slight shade of gray that tells me she may be ready to puke. While it's normal to be nervous on a first interview, in Coop's world it's not a good thing to wear those nerves on your sleeve.

"You okay, Miss Perez?"

"Fine. Just excited."

I knock on Coop's door and wait for him to answer instead of walking right in like I usually do. When he opens the door my mouth almost drops to the floor in surprise and maybe even in a bit of lust.

He's dressed in a freakin' suit. An expensive one at that. A custom fit, Italian made, steel gray suit with a white shirt and black tie.

He almost takes my breath away, and I'm not sure how it happened or when it happened. I've been looking at this same man for years. So why does he look like a completely different person to me at this moment?

"Jane, this is my employer Cooper Barnes."

"Pleased to meet you," she says eagerly. "I'm Jane Perez."

Coop lazily rakes his eyes up and down Jane's curvy frame. They settle on her breasts for a moment and then back to her face. It's quite obvious that he approves of the visual.

Shake it off, Ursula.

A small grin spreads across Coop's face.

"You don't know who I am, do you?" he asks sounding almost relieved.

Jane looks as if she isn't totally sure what she should say right now, but it's not my job to bail her out. I need to make sure she can handle herself—especially with Coop.

"No, I'm afraid I don't."

"Not a football fan?"

"No, not really. I'm more of a tennis girl."

"Who do you like?"

"Sir?"

"In tennis. Who do you like?"

"I like a lot of players, but I guess my favorites right now are Nadal and Federer."

"Ohh, the hot men of tennis."

Jane blushes.

Is she for real?

"You could describe them in that way, but what I love most about them is their game. They're true champions and give a hundred percent effort every time they're on the court."

"I guess somebody may see a few Wimbledon tickets in her future," Coop jokes.

There she goes blushing again.

And why is he trying to impress her?

"Tickets would be very much welcomed if they

come as a perk of the job."

"Well I'm not a tennis player, but I can definitely identify with being a champion. I've earned three Super Bowl rings and have been to five Pro Ball games," he boasts.

"Wow, that's quite an accomplishment for someone so young."

Coop peels off his jacket and lays it neatly on the back of his sofa. Then he starts rolling up the sleeves on his shirt bearing the ink on his forearms. Jane is doing a bad job of trying to avert her eyes from his thick, corded arms, although I'm not doing too much better either. I help myself to a bottle of water from Coop's mini refrigerator in an effort to swallow the massive lump that feels lodged in my throat.

"Would you like some water as well, Miss Perez?" I ask.

"No, thank you."

"I'd like some," Coop says with an intensity and tone he's never used with me before.

I grab another water as he silently watches my every movement. Then I hand it to him without saying a word. Feeling jittery the entire time.

"Thank you, Miss Owens."

"Mm-hmm."

"So ... Jane, just so you're clear about the job. I play

tight end for the New York Nighthawks which keeps me busy from July to playoff season. So, if we have a crappy season, I'm on six months and off six months but if we make it to the big dance, I'm on seven and off five. Either way those will be your busiest months, because when I'm playing football, it's the only thing I want to concentrate on."

"I need to know that there is someone handling everything else when I'm not around and handling it well. I own several businesses, and I'm about to open a private high school for boys in Brooklyn. You'd be managing all of my appointments, phone conferences, and correspondence. In other words, you have big shoes to fill."

"I look forward to learning all that Miss Owens has to teach, Mr. Barnes. I assure you that I will do my best to learn quickly and make this transition seamless for you."

"Awesome. So, tell me—" Coop glances at me then back at Jane. "Are you married, Jane?"

"No, Mr. Barnes." She almost giggles.

I CANNOT with her.

"Boyfriend?"

"I have no time for any of that, Mr. Barnes. I'm putting my little brother through school. He was born with a birth defect of the spine and isn't able to walk but is a whiz with computers. This is his freshman year in college."

Oh my God.

Kill me now.

Jane is a saint.

A saint with jugs.

"How do you work full time and take care of your brother?"

"My aunt is his companion, but I financially support the three of us."

"Very admirable."

"There wasn't even a question of what to do. Family takes care of family."

"Very true. So just one last thing, Jane, how we were so lucky to come across you for this position? Are you in between jobs?"

"My last employer said something derogatory about my brother's disability in a fit of anger. I could not work for her any longer. While I realize that things are said in the heat of the moment, I lost all respect for her. I can't work for anyone whom I can't respect."

Well good luck with that then.

"I love that!" Coop claps his hands together once loudly. "Let's give it try then, Miss Perez. You're hired."

My head is suddenly clouded with second thoughts.

What have I done?

"Owens, she can share your office."

Ugh.

COOP

"I demand to see the medical documentation proving that there is any therapeutic benefit to soaking our balls in ice water after every practice."

I'm in pissy mood.

Practice is over for the day and now it's time for NFL styled aftercare. Some players are stretching out, others are getting massages, but a few of us, including Saint and I, are taking our turns to sit and shiver to death in NFL approved cold water immersion tubs.

"I'm pretty sure there are hundreds of years of medical research supporting that, although there probably is a sadist in the afterworld somewhere laughing his head off at us."

"They should serve alcohol in here."

"I take it that you haven't let Owens sit on your face yet."

"I will shove your head down in this ice if you talk about her like that again."

Saint laughs out loud.

"Well, have you at least told her that she's a great assistant? Have you told her how much you appreciate how she always has your back? Have you told her that you don't want her to leave?"

"Not exactly."

"So, let me get this straight. You've never told her how valued she is?"

"Her paycheck tells her that."

"People need to hear the words. No wonder she wants to leave. And now that she is you still can't find the words to ask her to stay?"

"It's not that I want her to stay, I just want to understand why she's leaving."

"That sounds like the same thing to me. If you didn't care you wouldn't need to know."

"She knows how I feel."

It's just that she doesn't give a damn.

"You still seeing that Kiera girl?"

It's been a while since I've seen Kiera or any woman for that matter. I've been too preoccupied with figuring out what the hell is the matter with Owens.

"No, I've just been chilling. Getting my head right for the season."

The team doctor, Dr. Collingswood, comes by to check on us.

"How's the temperature, guys?"

"Frigid."

"Arctic," I add for emphasis.

"Well that sounds about right. Means all your muscle micro tears are healing."

The doc double checks the thermometer and the timer on the tub.

"You've got about five more minutes, fellas, and then it's time for your rub downs."

"Thank fuck."

"And by the way, Coop, everything looks good with your ear. No significant changes since last year. You should be all clear for the season."

"Thanks, doc."

The doctor moves on to the next tub of players.

"You know I've never pried into your private life, Coop."

"But it sounds like you're about to do just that."

"Well, we've known each other over five years, and you've never told me about what happened to your ear."

"There's nothing to tell. I was involved in an accident back in the day. The collision blew out part of my ear drum."

"Gotcha."

"Not the story you were looking for?"

"If you think for one minute that I believed those stories about Coach Barnes you must be crazy. I know your father is a good man. I was just curious. Even though you play around a lot, and have a good heart, you're very much a secret squirrel. Very guarded. It's hard to get to know you. It's difficult to talk to you. It's probably part of the reason why you had no warning that Owens was leaving. People feel as if they can't tell you anything. That you don't want to hear it or that you don't care. Maybe that's why you were blindsided."

"I am not the person who you're describing. That's not me."

"Aren't you? Think about your inner circle. There's me. Probably the only player on the team you talk to about stuff other than the game. And let's be honest, we first became friends because my brother asked me to look out for you when you came here."

"Thanks for that," I say sarcastically.

"You're welcome. And then there's Tito. Your personal driver who probably says five words out loud a day. Just the way you like it. And then there's the woman of the week. A few months ago, it was Megan. Last week it was Kiera. This week it will be someone else. You pick very, let's say, sexual women who you will never get serious about and could never bring home to your mother."

"Which is exactly the point."

"And then there's Owens. The dutiful assistant who spends the most time with you but probably knows you the least. If she did, she should have known that her exit wasn't going to be a smooth ride out of the door, but I don't think she knew that. I think she thought you wouldn't give a shit. That she was replaceable. That maybe you'd give her a bonus check, a good reference, and a nice knowing you."

Saint has the unique ability of making me think of things in a different way. Ways that make my head hurt.

"They really should start serving drinks in here."

"Have you said anything to Parinzino yet?"

"Hell no."

Paul Parinzino is Saint's new backup quarterback who is now sleeping with Megan and evidently taking her to award shows. I have no interest in talking to him unless he's throwing me a ball on game day.

"What a bitch."

"Him or her?" I snicker.

"Either of 'em." We both laugh. "But I'm not worried about Parinzino. I've never felt better. I'm going to crush it this season. He's not taking my spot anytime soon."

"It doesn't matter about Megan either. We were never exclusive. She can sleep with anyone she wants to. Even a teammate."

"That's so ridiculously sad I think I'm going to cry."

Saint pretends to rub phantom tears away with his hands.

A few of the players around us start laughing, so I have to get a jab in.

"Like the way I cried the day you handed over your manhood to Sabrina on your wedding day?"

I get a couple of *oohs* from the guys.

"Hey, I don't understand why you were crying for me. I get a home cooked meal and a blow job every night. What do you get?"

The therapy room fills with raucous laughter. Even

the strait laced Doctor Collingswood cracks a smile.

"You're such a jackass."

I flick an ice cube at his head.

"I'll take that as a compliment coming from you. Oh, by the way, guess what I heard?"

"Aren't you the fucking busybody this week?"

"It's about Owens," he singsongs.

Of course, that gets my immediate attention. I take the bait.

"What?"

"That guy Jim from The Examiner was overheard talking about her. Something about her fat ass."

"You're lying."

I can feel my pressure rising.

"Why would I lie? You think half of the team isn't looking at Owens when she comes to practice in those fucking tight workout pants and tiny T-shirts with no bra?"

"Who's looking at her?!" I yell to the room. "Who is looking at Owens?"

A couple teammates on my offensive line start slowly raising their hands. Belkin. Rand. Hobson. What the fuck?

"Sorry, but she's hot, Coop."

"Owens is not to be fucked with!" I bark.

"We know, dawg. That's why no one has."

"What else did Jim say?" I ask Saint.

"He's taking your girl to dinner this week."

"What?" I shake my head in disbelief. "It must have something to do with the interview I said I'd do. Owens doesn't date."

"Owens is doing a lot of things she didn't used to do."

"It's not a fucking date."

"Well, what else would you call it?"

"There's no way that she would give someone like him the time of day. I'm telling you this is all about that damn interview that I already regret agreeing to."

"Whatever you need to believe."

"Yo, what the hell is she doing?" I splash the ice water angrily with my fist.

"Hey, watch it!"

"She's confusing the fuck out of me. Maybe she has cancer or something?"

Saint gives me a screwed up face.

"First of all, why would you even say something so stupid like that. Owens does not have fucking cancer. You're grasping at straws. Quite desperately I might add."

"Well why else would she quit out of nowhere and consider going out with that douchebag. Maybe she's working on some sort of bucket list. Maybe she's—"

"Going to sit on his face this week?"

The entire room erupts in laughter, and before I can shove Saint's big mouth under the ice, the good doctor intervenes.

"Time's up, you two. You have thirty seconds to get to the massage room."

CHAPTER SEVENTEEN

URSULA

"Morning, everyone."

"Morning, Mr. Barnes!" Jane responds.

Tito just gives a head nod as usual and I respond ... cautiously.

"Good morning."

It's rare to find Coop in such a good mood this early in the morning. In fact, I'm going to go out on a limb here and say it's odd.

"Tito, I'm going by the school before practice today. Owens, you want us to scoop you up on the way back or do you want to take a car service there?"

"Wait ... what?"

"Jane and I are going to go by the school first. I just wanted to know if you wanted us to pick you up on the way to training camp or did you want to get there on your own?"

"Oh ... umm, it probably would be out of the way for you to come back and get me."

Tito stares at me thoughtfully then speaks.

"We could come get you," he asserts.

Coop checks his watch.

"Owens might have a point. I didn't think about all the traffic going in that direction on the bridge. It might be kind of tight. No telling who we may run into at the school either. I have a few things to go over with the builder, so why don't you just meet us at the field."

"Uh—okay."

Jane smiles at the both of us. Oblivious of the work ahead of her at camp. It's a delicate dance keeping the reporters at bay and keeping the fans happy. Especially when you work for one of the most popular players on the team. She's not even dressed properly for it.

"Sounds good. May I just run to the ladies' room before we leave, Mr. Barnes?"

"No problem."

As soon as she turns the corner toward the restroom, Coop leans in toward me.

"Jane's working out, huh?" he half whispers.

"Yes, she is," I try agreeing without showing any obvious attitude.

Tito walks quietly out of the room toward the kitchenette.

"You did good, Owens. She's a keeper."

"So, you trust her?"

"Until she shows me any differently, I think I know enough to comfortably hire her in your place. Don't you? She was your top choice, right?"

"Yes, she was my top choice."

Coop walks over to the large bay window in the common area and stares at the street below us with his back to me. I can't help but take a few moments to think about what my sisters would say if they were here at this moment. Coop may be a lot of things, not all of them good, but one thing I could never deny is that he is hot.

Today he's wearing a casual white tee and a pair of jeans that look like they were tailor fit for his physique. The simplicity of his outfit plays up the definition of his upper body and the sleek lines of his long athletic legs. His hair is loose and a bit messy which only adds to his laid-back sexiness.

"I realize that attending training camp has never been your favorite responsibility," he says still facing the window. "You can skip it today if you want."

"Skip it?"

"Yeah, might as well let Jane jump right in the deep end. That's how you learned." He turns to me. "Remember?"

I do remember. I was so nervous, so determined to do a good job, and constantly looking for Coop's approval.

"You're right, that is how I learned."

He moves closer to me, and I find myself stumbling a step or two back.

"Unless you want to go with us today?" he asks tentatively.

"If you want me to go I'll go. Whatever you need to make this easier for everyone."

"Easier." He parrots back the word almost as if it's almost ridiculous.

"Yes, easier."

He pauses for a moment then turns back around to the window. His demeanor completely nonchalant again.

"Well I don't think I need the two of you there today, so the *easiest* thing would be for Jane to go and for you to hang back."

My eyes almost well up.

"Fine."

"I'll talk to you later then."

"Sure ... I guess while the two of you are at practice, I can go to your house and make sure your food service is delivered for the week. Maybe put it away in the deep freezer for you."

"Thanks for that but I didn't want to bother you with work that the maid can easily handle. I should have never asked you to do that anyway, so I had her come in today to accept the deliveries."

"Oh." My voice cracks.

Finally, Jane returns from the bathroom.

"I'm ready, Mr. Barnes."

Coop abruptly turns to grab his things.

"Tito, we're ready!"

When the three of them walk away together and only Tito looks back at me, I feel a crushing pain in my chest. The ache takes me by surprise. I'm not sure if I'm being territorial, possessive, or what. The decision to leave was supposed to feel liberating, but all that it feels like at this point is freakin' lousy.

I'm beginning to accept the fact that I'm not an office girl. I guess I'm so used to traveling around with Coop and Tito, that I haven't spent much time sitting at a desk. I've never looked so forward to changing my clothes and having an early girls' night with my sisters as much as I do today. I need the mental break and the change of atmosphere.

"I love this restaurant. How did you find it?"

"It's one of my *find a man* spots. They have live music on Thursdays."

"Of course."

"So, how's our future niece or nephew doing in there?" I ask.

Carla pats her swelling stomach.

"I think he's hungry."

"That's the first time you called the baby a he."

"I just have a feeling lately that it's a boy."

"You have a feeling, or did you sneak and get the ultrasound done?"

"I assure you it's just a feeling. Dexter would kill me if I tried to find out the sex of the baby."

I do my best to hold my tongue when it comes to my sister's husband. He's a handsome man but a bit too controlling and opinionated for my taste. Monica on the other hand doesn't hold her tongue and checks him on a lot of stuff better than I ever could. I think he might be frightened of her.

"So, what's work like now that the new girl has started? Is your decision to go feeling a lot more real now?"

"Yep."

I start twisting my mother's ring around my finger while Carla stares at me thoughtfully.

"So she's working out?"

"Yeah, I think Coop likes her."

"Is she nice?"

"Uh-huh. Practically a saint."

Carla and Monica give each other a look.

"Is she pretty?"

"What does that matter?"

"It doesn't, I was just wondering."

"Yeah, she's pretty."

"You think Coop might be attracted to her?"

"What does that matter, Monica?"

I respond a little too harshly but neither one of my sisters even bats an eye. They just sit and wait for me to insert my own foot in my mouth.

"I mean she's definitely pretty, nice body, great disposition, but I don't think he likes her in *that* way. He's seeing someone, and Coop doesn't do that."

"Doesn't do what? Look at a pretty woman?"

The two of them laugh.

"Cheat."

"Oh ... is it cheating now to look? If that's the case, then Dexter can sue me for a divorce ten times over."

They both laugh again.

I take an angry bite of my chicken marsala and quietly chew.

"You seem a little sensitive about the subject, little sister. I thought this was something you wanted, or did you want your replacement to be butt ugly?"

More laughter.

Could I just toss a glass of water in their faces?

"It doesn't matter to me one way or the other. You two are annoying."

"Yep, we are."

"Oh crap, that's Dexter calling me. His meeting finished early. He's picking me up," Carla announces.

"What?! We just got here."

"We did not," she disputes. "We've been here for an hour. Gotta go and get my mandatory five o'clock bedrest."

"Well it's just us cool kids now."

"Yep."

"You want to go back to work?"

"Nope. There's literally nothing for me to do if I go back there."

"You want to get drunk?"

"*Hellz* yeah!"

Monica and I order a round of cocktails and a round of shots. About two drinks and one shot later the ache I was feeling has dissipated, and in place of it sits a warm glow that I wish I could feel all of the time.

"This must be why people drink," I say as I start sipping my third rum cocktail. Pinky in the air. Lips feeling a little tingly.

"You feeling no pain, little sister?"

"None at all."

"Me too. Wait, I gotta tinkle." Monica giggles. "You stay here."

Monica leans over when she stands up.

"Whoa."

"Can you make it, lightweight?" I tease.

"I got it. The bathroom is ... over there!"

My phone rings a few moments later.

It's him.

I think about just letting it ring, but a small part of my brain is still functioning with a little common sense. I still work for him for a few more weeks. I have to answer. I always answer.

"What," I answer curtly.

"Owens?"

"That's me!"

"Are you fucking drunk?"

COOP

"I don't get drunk, Mrrrr. Barnnnnes. I'm getting twwwisted!"

Owens is slurring every other word and laughing like I've never heard before. It's a higher pitched sound. It would be adorable if I wasn't so worried about her. If she's with that Jim guy, I will kill him. Literally.

"Where are you?" I demand to know. "Who are you with?"

"Since when do you care where I am or what I'm doing, you bad man."

I'm hopeful that her indignant words mean that my plan of gracefully accepting her resignation is working.

After listening to Saint, I've decided that my reaction to her leaving wasn't working in my favor and that maybe a change in attitude was required.

"What are you talking about, Owens?"

"What are you talking about Owens?" She tries imitating me using an exaggerated, deep voice.

"Stop mimicking me like a third grader and tell me what your problem is."

"You left me at the office today."

"I was training the replacement that you hired. Isn't that what you wanted?"

"You were trrrraining her, huh?"

"Yes, Owens."

"You like her, don't you?"

"Yes, I like her. I think she's going to work out if that's what you're asking."

"If that's what you're asking," she mimics me again. Her voice dropping even deeper.

I have to admit, it's a good imitation, and it's kind of funny. I guess she can do voices besides the ones she sees on television.

"You've been practicing that voice, haven't you?"

I can hear her take another gulp of whatever she's drinking.

"Shusssh your mouth, bad man."

I need to get to her.

"Where are you, Owens?"

"I'm out with people who love me. People who care about my well being."

"You're the one leaving me and now I don't give a shit? I'm not going to ask you again. Where. Are. You?"

I hear someone approach and interrupt our conversation.

It's a man.

I don't know Jim's voice, but I can only assume it's him. We'll see how much she wants to go out with him once I buy that crap shit paper he works for and fire his ass.

"Excuse me, miss, but I think the person who you're here with needs your assistance in the bathroom."

"Owens!"

"What? Stop yelling at me."

"Are you crying?"

"No."

I hear her sniffling.

"I'm sorry, darlin'." I calm down. "I just want to help. Who are you with?"

"My sister."

Thank fuck.

"Okay, go help your sister, but please hand your phone to the man you're talking to before you do."

"I don't want to give him my phone. You just bought me this phone."

I smile.

"Nothing will happen to the phone. Just please hand it to him. Okay?"

"Welllllll—"

Jesus Christ.

I wish she would just listen.

"Okay, I'll do it. I've gotta go to Monica now. I think her head is in a toilet."

Finally.

"Hello?"

"Thanks for grabbing the phone. May I please ask where you're located?"

"Seventh and seventy-second."

"And what is it?"

"The Blue Fish Grill."

"And do you work there?"

"No, I'm just having drinks here tonight, but my wife said that she thought your friend's companion might be in a little trouble in the bathroom. So, I came over to tell her."

"Why didn't your wife tell her?"

I don't trust him. Owens is drunk.

"Huh? Listen, man, my wife stayed in there with

the lady while I came over to inform your drunk friend. We're doing her a favor."

"Apologies, but the woman you were just talking to is someone very special to me. I trust that you can promise me that she'll be okay until I get there in about … let's say fifteen minutes."

"Now wait a minute—"

"My name is Cooper Barnes and there's something in it for you if you make sure that woman is sitting in her seat with a hot cup of coffee when I get there."

"Cooper Barnes? *The* Cooper Barnes."

"The one and only."

"Aww, man, it's nice to meet you. I never miss a game."

"Thanks for that. Listen, I'm going to change the estimated time of arrival. I'll be there in five. What's your name?"

"Bob McMillan."

"See you in five, Bob."

I hear them before I see them.

Owens and her sister have apparently made it back to their table and are holding court.

Grinning. Slurring. Laughing.

There are three men standing around their booth and none of them look at all like they are the married Bob McMillan.

When Owens notices that it's me literally flying through the door to get to her, her face lights up in a way that I don't think I've ever noticed before. Even drunk she's gorgeous. And my heart and my dick start pulsing.

"Coop!"

"Are any of you Bob McMillan?" I demand to know.

"Damn, are you that guy from the Nighthawks?"

"I'll be the guy who buys you your next round if you go drink it somewhere else."

"Sweet! No problem, CB. The ladies are all yours."

And that's how you clear out a room.

"Wow—is that all we're worth?" asks a woman who looks nothing like Owens, but who I assume is her sister.

"Yeah, you paid them off with an eight dollar drink." Owens chimes in. "I should have worn a sluttier dress."

It hasn't gotten past me that Owens is wearing a tight fitting, silver, strapless dress. It hugs her in all the right places, especially her ass.

"How many drinks have you had?" I ask her.

"I dunno ... how many drinks have you had?" She asks the question pointing a finger directly at my nose.

Yeah, she's definitely ten sheets to the wind.

I introduce myself to her sister for the first time ever. I'm not sure how that happened. That three years passed without me meeting one of Owens' family members. I guess I'm a little more self-absorbed than I thought.

"Pleased to meet you. I'm Cooper Barnes. Your sister's boss."

"The man. The myth. The legend."

They both start hysterically laughing.

"I take it Owens has said nice things about me?"

"Not even close. And why the hell do you call her Owens? Her momma named her Ursula. It's a beautiful name. She's not some player on your team. She's a woman with a name and she's my sister!"

The two of them high five each other.

"That's right!"

The bar starts playing Elton John's "Philadelphia Freedom" and all of a sudden Owens breaks out in song. I've never heard her sing a note in her life.

"This is my mom's song, Monica!"

"Philadelphia freedom shine on me. I love you. Shine a light ..."

All I can do is watch. I take a seat on one of the

wooden bar stools and listen to them sing the remainder of the song. They're horrible. Hitting flat notes. Totally off tempo. But I've never seen Owens look happier. And when I look around the bar, I can tell that a lot of other men see what I am seeing right now.

The light.

The glow.

That incandescent thing that some women simply have without even trying.

The shine that draws men toward them like a beacon.

I see a man at the end of the bar gathering the courage to approach. He's young. Scraggly beard. A hunger in his eyes. I stare him down until he understands.

Stay away.

Stay very fucking far away.

Another song comes on. This time it's Elton John's "Benny and The Jets."

Oh, hell no. I can't listen to another note. Light or no light.

"Okay, girls, it's time to call it a night."

I scoop her around the waist.

"Say good night, Owens."

"Good nnnight, Owens," she slurs back.

CHAPTER NINETEEN

COOP

"Noooo ... It's way too early, Mr. Barnes." Owens holds onto the sides of my shirt to keep her balance as I walk her back to the table to pay the tab and get the hell out of here. I like her tucked under me like this. She fits perfectly.

"Ewww, gross. No wonder he calls you Owens. It's because you call him Mr. Barnes. What's wrong with you two? You both act like you're Nana's age."

"She just started that mister nonsense," I say defending myself.

"Are you seeing Ariana Grande?"

The sister may be even drunker than Owens.

She's all over the place.

"Monica, I told you that wasn't true!"

"I know but you'd protect this man with your last earthly breath, so you might have been lying when you told me he wasn't."

I smile to myself.

Her last earthly breath?

"Okay, ladies, let's hit the road. Tito is waiting outside in the car for us."

"But I drove my car, Coop."

"You drove your car to the bar to get drunk?"

"Our designated driver had to leave early."

"I'll figure out a way to get your car home. You're leaving."

"You're gorgeous," Monica says to me with glassy eyes.

"Thank you."

"No seriously ... you're adorable on TV in your uniform and everything, but up close in those jeans your ass is everything."

They both bust out in spirited laughter.

I just shake my head.

"Come on you two and don't lag behind. I wouldn't want you to trip and fall staring at my perfect ass."

"And he's funny too? Wait until I tell Carla. You're an Aquarius, right?"

~

Tito and I agree that the best plan would be for him to drop Monica off at her house in Queens and for me to drive Owens home in her car to Brooklyn. I've never been in her car before, and I pray to God that I never will have to again. I practically have to fold my body in half to squeeze into the driver's seat.

"Why would you buy this tiny car?"

"It's a great car. Good on gas. Rearview camera."

"Look at me, Owens. If I pass out because of a lack of oxygen, it's because of this *great* car."

"Well this is all I could afford on my salary."

"Are you trying to say that I only pay you enough to afford half a car?"

She laughs loudly and rolls down the car window.

"This car is the perfect size."

"For a hobbit."

"Take me home, Jeeves!" she yells wildly with a faux British accent.

"What are you the queen mother now?"

"Yesss!"

Owens sticks her arm out of the window and holds it there as I zigzag our way through traffic. This is one thing that I've never really gotten used to about living in New York—the traffic.

It's like no one in this city ever goes the fuck home. There're always cars on the road. That's why I pay Tito to drive or else I'd probably have a panic attack. These are not normal driving conditions for any human being.

"I guess I don't pay you enough for you to live near the office either?"

"I do live near the office. It's near the bridge in Manhattan and I live on the other side of the bridge."

"In Brooklyn. Look at this traffic."

"Well, it doesn't matter. I don't work there anymore anyway."

"Even drunk you're a smart-ass."

"Am I drunk?"

The only good thing about Owens's car is that it's small enough to fit into practically any space. I easily park it in a small legal space in front of her building, and by the time I get out and come over to the other side of the car, I can see that she's wilting. The long car ride probably did her in and lulled her halfway to sleep.

"Upsy-daisy, Owens." I lift her up. "Come on."

She wraps one of her soft arms around my waist and leans into the side of my body as I guide her up the steps of her apartment. Tito and I have been here enough times to know where she lives even though I've never been inside.

"Third floor, right?"

"Fifth," she mumbles.

"Oh right. Fifth floor, apartment 503."

Her apartment is in an old five floor, walk-up building. No elevator. It figures that she lives on the top floor. I tell her to hold onto me and help her slowly up the stairs, because she has on heels and can barely see straight.

"You want to take off your shoes?"

"I'm not walking barefoot on these nasty stairs!" she says in horror.

Her eyes are half closed as she starts singing that song from the bar again.

"Philadelphia freedom ... I love ya. Shine the light."

"How do you know the words to that song? It's pretty old."

"My mom was from Philadelphia. It's where my parents met in college and fell in love. It was one of her favorite songs."

"Oh."

"My mom died a long time ago. I was really young. It's one of the only things that I remember for sure about her without other people having to fill in the blanks."

Owens starts tearing up. I didn't mean to bring up such a painful memory for her. The alcohol has her emotions are all over the place. I better get her to bed.

"I'm sorry about your mom, Owens. I can tell that you miss her."

"She was an awesome lady. Did you know that she was in a Burger King commercial?"

"No, I didn't know that."

"She was an actress."

"Wow, I didn't know that."

"Of course, you didn't, silly. You don't know anything about me."

That jab hurts a little, because she's wrong. She's so wrong.

"That's not true, Owens. I know a lot about you."

"Not the important stuff. Did you know that I'm an actress too?"

Her ankle suddenly turns.

"Ouch!"

"That's it," I say. Then I stand in front of her and crouch down. "Get on my back."

"Uh-uh."

"You're in heels, you just hurt your ankle, and we still have three floors to go."

"But I'll be too heavy."

"I'm in prime physical condition, Owens. I could carry your tiny ass across the country if I had to."

"Just this once."

She hikes up her dress, sliding her body onto my back, and wrapping her arms around my neck. She smells like roses and rum and warm pussy. This is going to be a long fucking night.

"So, finish what you were saying," I tell her to keep my dick distracted. "You're an actress."

"Oh, yeah, I'm an actress. I was a theater major in college."

"But you can't sing."

"Fuck you!"

I burst into laughter. I can count on my hand the number of times I've heard Owens use dirty words.

"You are so drunk," I say out loud.

"This is drunk?"

"This is definitely drunk."

"Then I like it." She laughs.

When we finally arrive, I help her inside of her apartment. An apartment that looks like a box of Crayola crayons threw up in. There's color everywhere. Figurines, wall art, accent pillows, stuffed animals. It's not what I expected, although to be perfectly honest, I'm not sure that I ever really gave much thought to what her apartment looked like inside.

"You want something eat?" she asks grinning widely as she kicks off her shoes. One of them goes flying into an oversized planter. I duck when she kicks off the other one.

"I'm not hungry but maybe you should eat something to sop up some of that liquor."

"Am I drunk?"

I laugh again.

"Yes, darlin', you're definitely drunk."

I start opening kitchen cabinets to look for something I can cook, because I don't see any bread, which is what she really needs.

"Do you ever go food shopping? What the hell are you eating every day?"

I turn for her answer and notice that she's stuck. She's sitting on the edge of her couch, trying to lift her tight dress up over her head and is stuck. It would be one of the funniest things I've seen in a long time if she was wearing a fucking bra and not wearing a white lace thong.

"Dammit, Owens, would you stop flashing your tits all of the time."

I rush over to her and lift her dress completely off. Might as well since she was halfway there. Her head full of large black corkscrew curls are all over the place, her eyes are half closed, and there's a huge goofy grin across her face.

"Wouldn't it have been easier to step out of it," I say taking a deep breath. Willing my dick to go down to its normal size.

"I'm so hotttt!" she slurs.

Yes, the fuck she is.

"Hold this against your boobs please and go change. Why isn't your air on anyway? It's definitely hot in here."

I can't avert my eyes from the jiggle her ass cheeks make as she walks toward her bedroom.

"I'm never here," she answers once inside the bedroom. "I can't have that thing running all day."

"I think I pay you enough to cover the electric bill."

"It's not about whether or not I have the money. It's about common sense."

She walks back out into the living room wearing a Harry Potter pajama tank top and matching shorts. Now this is something I'd expect from her. Totally quirky. Totally Owens.

"It's about not taxing the resources of—"

"Blah, blah, blah," I say cutting her off. "You talk entirely too much when you're drunk."

She walks over in what I think is an attempt to hit

me in the chest, but completely misses the mark. I thought the liquor was wearing off, but maybe not. I think she still sees two of me.

I quickly catch her with one arm.

"Oops." She giggles.

And then ... the last fucking thing I need happens.

CHAPTER TWENTY

COOP

She touches me.

She touches me, and it sets every single nerve ending in my body on fire.

"Even your muscles have muscles," she coos as she rubs one of my forearms.

"You like muscles?" I ask through clenched teeth.

I've never considered the type of man that Owens would like, because I've never even heard her talk about dating. Now all of a sudden, I'm curious as fuck.

"Uh-huh."

"What else do you like?"

"Hair!" she states emphatically.

My eyes partially close as she strokes some of the

strands of my loosely pulled man bun. I find myself hoping that I possess everything she likes.

"What else?" I growl.

I pick her up to sit her up on the kitchen counter away from me while I cook. I need her to stop touching me, but she wraps her arms around my neck as I lift her.

"Protection," she murmurs way too closely by my ear.

My dick gets even harder. In a minute, I'm going to be in agony. Blue balls type of agony.

"I can do that."

"You can do what?"

I sit her down on the cool granite. Should I answer her again? What am I doing right now? She's totally wasted. She won't even remember this conversation tomorrow.

"Ooh, that feels much better. Did I tell you that it's hot in here?"

"Uh, I'm in this apartment with you. I can tell it's hot as hell in here too." I laugh.

"So whatcha going to cook?"

"Pasta with olive oil, garlic and tomato sauce. It's all you have in here."

"I have all of that?"

"Yep, and if you had a pie crust in here, I could even make you a tomato pie. That's my specialty."

"You can cook, Coop?"

Back in Georgia, I used to cook all the time for the family when my mother had to work late or had a parent teacher meeting. I'm actually a pretty good cook. Owens has worked for me all this time and didn't know that?

"I can cook, and this shit is going to taste like a gourmet meal."

"You're a riot," she says with some sort of indiscernible accent. I think she's trying to imitate a 1940s gangster.

"What's funny about me?"

"You think you're so good at everything."

"It's a gift and a curse."

"You're not good at everything though."

She starts swinging her legs back and forth like a big kid. Her heels thump against the cabinet doors. I've never seen her so relaxed. It's a dick move, but this is probably the only opportunity I'm going to get to find out what she's actually thinking. Why she's leaving me.

"What am I not good at, Owens?"

"You don't call your mother enough, you're a bad communicator, and you have commitment issues."

I toss the ingredients into the only large skillet that seems to be in her cabinet.

"I spoke to my mother just last night."

"You never stay with one woman for longer than six months."

"I've never met a woman that warranted sticking around any longer than that."

"I don't think you'd know if you met her."

She leans her head against the spice cabinet.

"I feel dizzy."

I turn off the pot.

"Come here, Owens."

I reach out my arms and she falls against my body inside of my embrace. When my hair accidentally comes out of the top knot it was in, she begins to mindlessly run her hands through it while I carry her to her bedroom. I stop mid stride for a moment and close my eyes.

"What are you doing?" I demand to know between labored breaths.

"Your hair is beautiful, Coop."

I start to wind one of her curls around my finger.

"So is yours."

"Why are we stopping?" she asks.

I lift her up, silently motioning her to wrap her legs around my waist. Then I lean her against the wall right outside of her bedroom. If I did this inside of that room, I might not want to stop. If I do this right here, it will just be one stolen moment.

I move my lips in closer to hers. Staring at her doe-like, expressive eyes when I do. Making sure she's totally awake and aware of what's going on. *The liquor has to be wearing off a little at this point* is how I rationalize this very bad decision I'm making.

"I've wanted to do this all night."

"Wanted to do what?" she whispers.

"This."

I kiss her lips softly at first. Being careful not to be too excited about it. I don't want to scare her to death. I pull back a bit then nibble at her lower lip. Coaxing her for a response. Maybe to even lead.

And then she slides one of her hands into the back of my hair, gripping it at the roots, and deepening our kiss. I moan softly inside of her mouth as my tongue explores every inch of it.

It takes every ounce of self restraint I have not to take this further. Especially when her bed is two steps away. I slow things down and then finish the kiss. Both of us breathing heavily afterward. She's staring at me with an intensity that seems almost foreign to her. Like she's angry and horny. That shit is a total turn-on.

"That kiss was nothing like I imagined," she says with a dead serious look on her face. Still in my arms.

"You imagined us kissing?"

She doesn't answer that and lays her head on my shoulder. Her arms and legs still wrapped around me.

"I'm sleepy, Coop." She yawns.

I walk us inside of her bedroom and find more color. Burnt orange walls, mismatched wooden bedroom furniture, and pictures of her family framed in assorted colored photo frames. It's at this moment that I truly understand that I don't know as much about Owens as I thought I did, and there is proof of that sad fact all over her house.

She loves color. She's not the neatest person in the world. She never cooks. She's into astrology? There's a large poster on her wall detailing the many attributes of a Gemini. She collects things. Art. Figurines. Buddhas. Dream catchers. Jewelry boxes. Pictures of wildlife. I'm drawn immediately to the large poster she has hanging of one lone wolf with haunting green eyes.

I smile when I see that some of her collectibles are from places that we've traveled to together: Florida, California, London. Others are from places that she's probably never traveled to but wants to visit: Bali, Australia, Alaska.

It's obvious that she loves her family. There are

pictures of them all over the walls as well. A picture of her parents. She looks exactly like her mother. A newer picture of her dad with who I assume is his new wife. There's another photo that includes a large group of people at what looks to be Owens' college graduation. They all look so happy, especially her.

Owens' eyes are closed and her mouth wide open when I lay her gently down on the bed. There's a quilt with a large dreamcatcher design on her bed. I don't pull it over her legs, because it's still pretty warm inside of her apartment. I turn on her ceiling fan, and hope that she doesn't sweat to death before her window unit has a chance to cool the room down.

An indescribable urge comes over me in the moment. She looks so peaceful. So beautiful. I bend down to gently stroke some strands of her hair.

"Pleased to finally meet you, Ursula Owens," I whisper softly in her ear. Then I place one chaste kiss on her forehead. "Don't go anywhere just yet. We're just getting to know each other."

CHAPTER TWENTY-ONE

URSULA

It's been a long seven days. I'm still spending most of my time training Jane, hating Jane, and then girl-crushing hard on her again. She's a really sweet girl and it's unfair that I'm taking some of my stuff out on her. It's just that I'm seriously confused and conflicted since I drunk kissed my boss.

Coop has been busy with football or plans for the high school, so we've been like two ships passing in the night. It's probably for the best though, because it makes it a lot easier to avoid him for the next few weeks that I have left here.

If the kiss meant anything to him, he wouldn't be

radio silent like this. He would have brought it up or something. Wait, what am I saying? A kiss has never meant anything to him. I'm going to chalk the whole thing up to a drunken mistake. I'm allowed to make at least one of those in a lifetime.

I haven't taken a day off of work since Carla's last miscarriage. That was over a year and a half ago. I suppose it would be safe to say that I have used work these past years to fill my life with meaning when I should have been trying to find joy in other places. So that's what I'm going to do over these next two weeks. Focus on me. Find my joy.

Today's theme is total relaxation. Something I've always believed isn't in my DNA, but that I'm going to try today. First up is a forty-five minute Swedish massage by a gorgeous Greek masseuse named Nikos. Too bad he's gay. Twenty minutes in and I think my Greek god wants to strangle me. I had no idea that I was this ticklish. Massages are not for me.

Next up is a hot stone pedicure and a gel manicure. These go swimmingly well. Both my nails and toes are a soft pink color which pops against my rich summer tan.

I can't get Greece off the brain, so I stop at a food truck and order a gyro. It's delicious. There's nothing like food truck cuisine.

Next up is the hair salon. I decide that today I'm going to do a length check and get my curls blown out, trimmed, and colored. I want the works. Carla sends me the name of her stylist who is about twenty minutes where I'm from and has a last minute cancellation.

Aside from the massage, I feel like my day is going pretty well. I think I could get used to a routine of self-care. The stylist offers me a hand mirror after ninety minutes of primping and prodding, cutting and coloring.

"How do you like it?"

I take a look in the mirror and fall in love with the woman in the reflection.

"It's perfect."

My hair feels lush and healthy and is dyed the perfect warm chestnut brown with a few strawberry-blond highlights. No more harsh black color. The stylist blew it out, trimmed the ends, and then gave me loose beach waves with a few flicks of a large barreled curling iron.

"Glad you like it. I'm trying to get your sister to get some highlights after she has the baby."

"That's a good idea. She'd look great."

My phone hasn't rung once and I've purposely avoided checking emails. If anything really pressing were to come up, I'm sure Jane would call me right away for some assistance. All must be well. It's not easy for me, but I have to learn how to let go and be in the moment. I need to learn how to follow this new path that I'm on—wherever it may lead.

Before I head home, I decide that it might be a nice idea to take a stroll around my neighborhood while catching up on one of my favorite podcasts on acting. I'm about thirty minutes away from my apartment when the sky becomes overcast and billowy, gray clouds start to roll in.

The meteorologist I watched on the news this morning should get a pay cut. She hasn't predicted the correct weather in the last three weeks. At this point I think that meteorology might be a complete sham. Just like astrology.

I quicken my steps, because I don't want a thunderstorm ruining my beautiful beach waves. It's Thursday and the plan was to forget about that kiss by putting on a little red lipstick, some tight jeans, and hanging out with Monica for once. I at least wanted to show her my sexy hairdo before it turns into one giant frizz ball.

My body trembles at the sound.

Thunder.

Thunder that I can feel deep inside my chest.

Thunder that sounds eerily familiar and triggers a deep-seated fear in me that I can't explain.

The thunder of my dreams.

The drops start to fall and are as heavy and punishing as a spray from a backyard water hose. Powerful. Heavy. Cool.

I start to run.

My one hundred fifty dollar hairdo starts to fall and quickly sticks to the sides of my face. My sundress is drenched. My Converse are soaked. I run faster.

The thunder rumbles again.

And now lightning follows it.

Cracking the sky wide open and triggering a memory I had long believed was dormant forever.

I stop where I am and collapse on a set of concrete steps. Huddled into a ball. Reliving a nightmare under the clouds and the rain.

I remember.

Metal bending at the mercy of more metal.

The taste of blood and tears.

We were hit.

A car plowed into the back of ours. I can't picture it exactly. I just know that there was another car involved and it hit us with enough brute force that my mother went flying forward, hitting her head on the steering wheel.

I, on the other hand, wasn't wearing my seatbelt. I was hiding on the floor of the car from the storm. So, I went flying sideways, banging my head against the backseat door.

And now I remember the pain.

Sharp, excruciating, pain.

Being tossed like a rag doll as my mother and I flipped over and over in the car, all I could remember hearing were the sounds of my own screams.

And then there was utter silence.

The crash probably occurred in less than a span of sixty seconds, but it seemed like an eternity to me. Like a deep sea diver who sometimes loses his bearings when he's low on oxygen, I was lying on the inside roof of the car and completely disoriented.

I called for my mommy.

But she didn't answer back.

I was frightened and thought she was asleep or maybe that she left. I didn't know. It was dark and there wasn't much I could see. Maybe I was dead.

I remember feeling sleepy and a little nauseous, so I thought it might be best to close my eyes for a while. Trusting that my mommy would come for me when she could.

Then I felt tugging on my arms. Someone was pulling me. It hurt.

"Wake up," the voice ordered. "Wake up, little girl."

The voice was small but steady. Telling me to hang on as he pulled me out of the car and onto the side of the road by the river. It was still raining hard. So hard the droplets were hurting my head. The boy held me for a minute. Covering me with his body.

"Sit here for a minute," he told me.

"My mommy." I remember saying.

"One of the grown-ups will get her out. I'm sorry but I can't do it."

I began to cry.

There were other cars turned in various positions on the roadway behind us. We weren't the only ones this happened to.

"Wolf!" I could hear a woman calling that name. Almost crying. She was calling for the boy who was holding me. "Where are you, Wolf?"

"I gotta go. The firemen are here. Don't worry. They'll get your mom out."

"Wait."

"I'll come back for you, all right? Sit right here. Don't move and they'll help you."

I cry when he leaves.

I'm crying right now.

Wolf.

The boy who pulled me to safety.
I gasp at the recollection.
I think his name was Wolf.
And I think I recognize the face.

CHAPTER TWENTY-TWO

COOP

"I have to tell you that I was pleasantly surprised that you called me, Mr. Barnes. I didn't think you were actually going to agree to this interview, much less be the one to initiate it."

"I guess all those days you've spent sitting on the bleachers cozying up with Owens didn't help with your understanding of me. Didn't she communicate that I'm a man of my word?"

Jim the reporter looks at me contemplatively.

"We don't talk about you much," he says with a cautious smirk.

Motherfucker.

We both sit down, directly across from each other,

in some sort of homemade lounge set up in *The Examiner* offices.

"Speaking of Ursula, is she coming today? I know she usually likes to attend most press events, and since she did have an indirect hand in making this happen, I'd hoped she'd be here."

I bet you did.

"She won't be joining us today but while we're on the topic of … *Ursula* … I just wanted to get something straight with you."

"And what is that?"

"She's off limits. Meaning she can't engage in any personal relationships with staff. It's a direct conflict of interest. You understand."

Jim stares at me with a cocky grin.

"I don't work for you, Mr. Barnes."

"You work The Nighthawk beat, I am a franchise Nighthawk player, and Owens works for me. Therefore, it's a direct conflict of interest."

"I don't think it is, and until she tells me differently, I'd prefer it if you'd stay out of my and Ursula's private affairs. You know … I just wouldn't want to make things awkward for her."

I sit back in the large leather club chair I'm sitting on and lift my legs up on the matching ottoman. Jim is determined to get under my skin and while I should probably get up and leave now, I want to see where this is headed. What's his angle?

"Maybe we should get started," I say.

"Awesome. Can I get you anything?"

"I'm good. Let's just get this over with."

"Fine by me. Like I said, I appreciate you taking the time out of your very busy schedule."

He says that like it's a federal crime that I work.

"Just so you're aware, Mr. Barnes, I'll be taping this conversation for reference purposes, fact checking, etcetera."

"I figured as much."

There are a few things about Jim that rub me completely the wrong way. He talks too much about Owens. He acts like he knows her so well when I know that cannot be the case. Secondly, he's cocky to a fault. He has some sort of chip on his shoulder. If I had to guess it's because he played football in high school, loved it, but sucked at it and now he hates all of us who are fortunate to make a living at it. Lastly, he's ambitious and not in the healthy way. I think he'd sell out his own mother to get ahead in his career.

"Readers love to hear about their favorite players' hometown roots. Could you tell us a little bit about your life in Georgia?"

"Georgia is one of my favorite places in the world.

The only way to really describe it is that it's a place I think about when I'm thinking of good food, good people, and home."

"You were raised there your entire life?"

"Born and bred. I never lived anywhere else until I came to New York as a rookie."

"Your life in Georgia seems a lot different than your life now in New York. How do the two compare?"

Where is he going with this shit?

"New York is my new home, and I love it in different ways. It's where my fans are, it's where my businesses are, and it also has a great community of people. Just a lot more of 'em."

"Do you think you'd ever leave the Nighthawks for a different team?"

"There's only but so much control you have over your career in the NFL. If the team wants to trade me at some point, they will, and there won't be much I can do about it."

"Except maybe buy the team."

We both laugh uncomfortably, but I don't respond to that comment. There's been talk about me investing in a NFL franchise for some time, but nothing has materialized. It's just been a few conversations here and there.

The reality is that owners don't want to see players gain ownership, especially young ones like me who know players on every team and who have relationships with those players. It would be bad for business.

"It's been said that the only situation where the team would ever consider trading you would be to make room in the budget to draft some of the missing pieces in the offense. Maybe defense too. Would you consider taking a pay cut to allow room in the budget to get what the Nighthawks need?"

He might as well just say I should play for free. Yeah right, that shit isn't happening. I put my body on the line every season to try and bring this city a championship. I should be compensated for that whether or not I'm already rich or not.

"I actually think we look damn good this year. Definitely playoff contenders. We're not missing much, so I guess that's not something I need to worry about in the near future."

He scribbles down some notes on a notepad.

"How are you feeling so far about the trades made over the summer? There's a new backup quarterback in town and his name is Parinzino."

"I don't know much about him yet, but I'm sure he will be a great addition to the team. I look forward to seeing what he can actually do. I hear that he has had very little actual time on the field."

Coach is going to make me pay for that passive aggressive comment.

"Umm ... that's a good point you make." Jim's eyes light up. He thinks he's got me right where he wants me. I took that one jab at Parinzino, but it won't happen again. "Do you know if Saint Stevenson is getting to know him? Mentoring him on handling the pressures of being a prime time quarterback?"

"It's not Saint's job to mentor Parinzino, it's his job to win ball games, but I can't speak for either of them. I'm sure they're handling Nighthawk business like we always do."

"Like a well oiled machine."

"That's right."

He jots down a few more notes.

"I think it's fair to say, Mr. Barnes, that you've had some distractions over the years. A few Twitter wars. Several bar fights. A discrimination case at one of your pizzerias."

What a bad segue.

"That's old news, Jim."

"Fair enough, but—"

"If it's a fair point then why are you bringing all of that old shit up?"

"Trust me it's leading somewhere. I'm just wondering if perhaps your past trauma may explain some of the drama to the fans."

My stomach drops. He knows.

"What past trauma?"

"Well, Mr. Barnes, it's a matter of record that you were abducted in your hometown in Georgia when you were just ten years old."

I clench my fists.

"Held for five days and even taken across state lines to New York."

"Turn the recorder off."

"Only for divine intervention to step in and save you, when you and your abductor were involved in a car crash on the FDR drive."

"That shit is not public record."

"I'm sure your family paid to have your records sealed, but if you dig deep enough there are ways to unearth any case file. No paper trail is ever really destroyed."

I stand up.

Fuming.

My breaths are rapid and harsh.

I want to lash out. I want to hurt someone. I want to hurt Jim.

"I know you may be angry right now, but I'm not

trying to blindside you, I'm just trying to tell your story in your words."

"That's not a story I have ever wanted to tell."

"Why? You could inspire so many victims. Look at what happened to you and look who you are today."

"That's not your call to make. That's not why I agreed to this interview."

"Well I could have just reported this without your input or your approval. I'm just trying to be respectful."

"You think you're being respectful? You think you're doing me some sort of fucking favor?"

"I don't understand why you're being so secretive about this. Because you were abducted? Because a woman did it? You were a kid. It wasn't your fault."

"You little shit. This is my business. My story to tell or not tell. It's not up for discussion now or at any time unless I say it is. If you publish it, I will sue you and your dime store paper. You won't be able to get a job at any news outlet in this country. In fact, you'd be lucky if you can get a job teaching English to first graders in a third world country."

We stare each other down.

"The story will run," he says matter of factly.

I approach him in a threatening manner. Towering over him by height and width.

"You're fucking with the wrong person, *Jimmy*."

"And so are you. Ursula is smart enough to make her own decisions about who she wants to date, and I'm smart enough to know a good story when I see one."

"This is your last warning."

Especially when it comes to Owens.

I'm not to be fucked with.

CHAPTER TWENTY-THREE

URSULA

I'm sitting in the common area thinking about what I've remembered in addition to what I've learned over the last twenty-four hours. There's a lot to digest.

"What do I have on the books today, Owens?"

I look up at my boss in wonderment and ask myself if I ever knew this man at all.

"Three meetings at eleven, one and then four p.m."

"Cancel them."

"All of them?"

"Yep."

"Why, what's up?"

"I have a last minute lunch meeting."

"With who?"

"A friend of mine from Los Angeles."

"You have friends?"

"Very funny, smarty."

"Okay, I'll take care of it. Is there anything else I can get you?"

Coop cocks his head to the side.

"You're acting weird being all helpful and shit."

"I'm your assistant. I'm paid to be helpful." I smile.

"You've got that goofy smile on your face. You're definitely being weird."

"No, I'm not."

"Yeah, you are. What's wrong with you today?"

"Nothing."

"Come here."

He pulls me toward him with a hungry look in his eyes. For a moment I think he's going to kiss me again, but then he stops, and only gives me a hug. It's a great hug though. And he smells delicious.

"What about Jane?" I whisper as he holds me a little longer.

"I don't care. I haven't seen you in a while," he says softly by my ear. "I missed you."

I hesitate for a moment and then I say it. "I missed you too."

Coop pulls me away from him, holding me firmly by my shoulders with a confused look on his face.

"Spill it."

"What?"

"Owens, you have to be the worst liar I've ever seen. Tell me right now what's going on."

Jane exits my office and interrupts us.

"Hey guys I'm going on a bagel run. There's a new bakery next door that makes gluten free ones. Would you two like anything? I heard they make amazing bagels, muffins and scones there."

"No thank you, Jane. Coop doesn't do baked goods during the season, and I'm going to pass too."

She looks mortified.

"Oh my God, I forgot about your strict eating regimen during the season. Looks like I have a lot more to learn. I apologize."

"Not a big deal."

"I'll be back in literally ten minutes."

"No problem, Perez. Go ahead. We don't punch a clock here."

After Jane leaves, I turn to go to my office. I want to say something to Coop about what's going on with me, but I don't know how to say it because when I do, it will change everything.

"I'm not going to ask you again, Owens. What the

hell is going on? You're quitting on me, you're going on dates with reporters, you kiss me then pretend like you didn't for days—"

I stop and turn around to face him.

"I kissed you?"

"Of course, you did. You couldn't help yourself."

"That's not how I remember it."

"How much do you really remember about it all? Maybe you need your memory refreshed."

"Maybe I do." I flirt.

"Oh, that's it ... something is definitely fucking up."

"I talked to Jim."

"What did that prick say?" he demands to know, practically spitting nails.

"He said quite a bit, but what I want to know from you is did you have a nickname as a kid?"

"Did I what?"

"A nickname."

He nods his head no.

"I need you to be honest with me?"

I grab his hand.

It's warm and large and calloused.

I slide my fingers through his.

"What was your nickname?"

"Fuck me," he mutters. Then he kisses my knuckles and then finally starts talking. "Football was my saving grace; it got me to come out of my shell because when I was a kid I was a loner. That's why my family used to call me the lone wolf or just wolf."

I squeeze his hand.

It's him.

The wolf from my dreams.

I don't know it just because of the things that Jim and I discussed, but because there's something about Coop's face that is so familiar to me all of a sudden.

"But your reporter friend and I didn't talk about that. How do you know that, Owens?"

"When I was a little girl I was in a car accident," I tell him.

"With your mother. I know."

"There was a storm and lots of thunder and lightning. I was frightened, so I took my seat belt off in the car and crouched down on the floor behind my mother's seat."

Coop starts to pull his hand away. I can already see that he knows what I'm going to say. I won't let him off that easy though. I firmly grip his hand. In fact, I hold onto it for dear life.

"No one knew at first that I was even in that car. There were so many cars involved in the crash and it took a while for first responders to get to us. But one person did. One boy."

"Owens—"

"And his name was Wolf."

"That has to be a coincidence."

"I don't think it was." I stare up into his smoldering, green eyes. "I think it was you."

"Is that the reason why you're giving me all of those adoring looks today? I thought it might have been because of what happened between us last weekend, but it's because you think I was the person who pulled you out of the car?"

"I'm just glad to have finally found you. So I can say thank you. Thank you so much."

He walks away from me and toward the bay window. Staring at all the people below us or maybe staring at nothing at all.

"It wasn't me."

"Now before you do something silly, like continuing to deny it, there's something else you should know. I looked back at your old employment records. There were a lot of applicants for my position."

"Yeah, so?"

"So, most of them had business degrees, all of them had prior experience as an executive assistant, and one had even worked briefly for Tom Cruise."

"And?" he says almost angrily.

"And you hired me. The acting major from a low ranked university with zero experience."

He presses his hands against the window pane.

Hanging his head low.

I walk behind him placing my palms against his back. Then I slide them around his waist.

"Why did you do that for me, Coop?"

He exhales heavily then breaks free from my embrace.

"I didn't."

URSULA

Jane and I have started to fall into an almost symbiotic rhythm at the office. I tell her what I'm working on and without me even having to ask, she starts working on assignments to support me.

If I'm talking to the builder about supply figures, she double checks behind me by searching our records for previous orders. If I say that it's almost time for Coop's lunch, she's already pulled out a couple of menus from restaurants that he hasn't eaten at in the last two weeks.

She even has the ratio of his protein smoothie down. He drinks it every morning and it has to be just right. Two scoops of protein powder, one large scoop of peanut butter, one banana, toss a few chia seeds in, eyeball the almond milk and then blend.

She also doesn't miss a beat.

She notices almost immediately that there's something not quite right between me and Coop. He walks by and barely says two words to us.

"Is Mr. Barnes in a bad mood today?" she asks. Her voice low.

"I don't know what's wrong with him," I say pursing my lips. "It's none of my concern."

"Well I guess it's just as well. You only have one more week do deal with his mood swings. I bet you're excited. Not about his mood swings but about embarking on a new chapter of your life."

"Totally," I deadpan.

I reconsidered going to training camp about thirty times before I finally came to the big girl conclusion that I wasn't going to avoid Coop any longer. I did nothing wrong.

I'm going to continue to do my job to the best of my ability until the very last day, and if he doesn't want to admit to the obvious truth of our converged pasts, then I'm not going to push him.

Maybe I did more harm than good revealing to him that I know he's the wolf. Maybe I brought up memories that he doesn't want to own or rather forget.

"Hi, Ursula."

"Hey, Jim."

"You're arriving a little late today."

"Yeah, I wasn't sure if I was going to make it here."

"Your guy looks like a beast out there today. He's ripping the defense apart."

"Is he now?"

I've decided that Jim and I are indeed friends. Dinner with him was no love connection, but it was nicer than I thought it would be. We talked about our favorite authors, our childhoods, and debated the finer points of Marvel Comics versus DC Comics. He's a decent enough guy.

A guy, who once I told him about my accident as a kid, recognized that there were glaring similarities to an accident that Coop had as a kid. An accident that Coop has never talked about publicly or privately—at least to me. An accident that explains why he prefers having a driver rather than drive himself around in New York; why he probably distrusts most women, why he lost part of his hearing when he was a kid, and why he hired me—the most unqualified applicant in the pile.

I was totally floored after that conversation with Jim. Speechless. Dumbfounded. The man I've been working for all these years isn't who I thought he was. He's not a selfish, self-absorbed egomaniac. He's not a spoiled, rich athlete. What he is...is an enigma.

While only a child himself, he bravely pulled me out of a car wreck. Then as an adult, he clearly hired me *on* purpose. He did things that seem so out of character for the person that I thought I'd been working for. The question is why did he do these things for me? Of course at this rate, I'm not sure I'll ever learn those answers. Coop seems quite determined not to tell me anything.

"I think he might hurt himself or one of his own teammates if he keeps it up at this rate," Jim comments.

"They'll be fine. It's just Coop being Coop."

I cue up my playlist of Earth, Wind and Fire to take my mind off of what's going down on the field. Coop definitely seems like he's on a self-destructive warpath today, but unfortunately there isn't much that I can do about it. I don't know why he's so worked up anyway. All I wanted to do was thank him.

Jim takes the seat next to me and leans across me to

extend a handshake to Jane who's sitting on the other side of me.

"Hi, we haven't formally met, but I've seen you here a couple of times and wondered who you were. My name is Jim McKinney, and I work for *The Examiner*."

Oops, did I not introduce them to each other? They'd actually make a cute couple.

"Pleased to meet you, Jim. I'm Jane Perez. Mr. Barnes new assistant."

"Oh ... I didn't realize. Ursula, are you leaving?"

Jane puts her hand over her mouth.

"I'm sorry. Did I speak out of turn? I apologize."

"It's fine," I snap.

I think that I may have hurt Jane's very fragile feelings, so she decides to make a trip to the concession stand to give me some space. I start to pop my earbuds back in when Jim continues talking.

"When were you going to tell me you were quitting?" he asks in an accusatory tone.

"I didn't realize that I had to tell you."

"Don't bite my head off too. I just thought ... we had dinner the other night. We talked about *a lot*."

"You're right, we did. It just didn't come up, Jim. Sorry."

"No problem. I just ... never mind. What are you listening to today?"

"Earth, Wind and Fire."

I show him the playlist I'm listening to on my phone.

"You have such eclectic taste in music."

"I think I got it from my mom."

"Can I listen? My dad loved this song too."

I hand Jim an earbud but before he has a chance to place it in his ear, a football comes soaring through the air and hits him smack dead in the middle of his forehead.

"*Oof!*"

"Oh my goodness!" a spectator exclaims. "Are you all right?"

The two old timers, who always sit up front, turn and try desperately to hold in their laughter and now I see why. Coop is staring over at us like a fire breathing dragon.

This was no accident.

I stare him back down for a moment and hope that he feels the eyes of shame that I'm trying to give him. Then I turn to check on Jim.

"Are you okay?"

"I'm fine, everyone," he says holding his palm to his

head where there's a dark pink knot starting to form. "It was just a football."

Jane returns from the stand with a popcorn in her hand. "What happened?"

"Can you reach into my cooler and hand me the frozen water bottle I have in there?" I ask her.

"Sure, thing."

I wrap the bottle in a few paper napkins and hand it to Jim.

"Here put this on your head to stop the swelling."

"Thanks, Ursula." He smiles in an obvious attempt to mask the embarrassment he must be feeling right now.

I notice that Saint Stevenson and the offensive coordinator are both speaking quite animatedly in Coop's face. There's no doubt they are reprimanding him for the hit. It was totally out of character for him and a juvenile thing to do. They're also trying to stop him from approaching us here in the bleachers, but that's the thing about Coop—nobody can stop him from anything when he's determined or delusional.

He walks right over to Jim.

"Sorry about that, man. I was trying to show Saint something and the ball slipped."

Translation: I meant to hit you and I dare you to say something about it.

Jim glares at Coop while holding the frozen Fiji water to his head.

"No problem, Barnes (he says without the Mr.). I know it wasn't done on purpose."

Translation: You did that totally on purpose, jackass.

"Jane ... Owens are you two okay?" he asks us both.

"Totally fine, Mr. Barnes," Jane answers. "The ball didn't hit anyone but poor Mr. McKinney here."

Coop picks up the football that he threw.

"Guess I'll give this away. Owens, can you give me a Sharpie?"

I roll my eyes while I hand him a marker. Coop signs the ball, and hands it to one of the kids sitting closest to us.

"Here you go, kid."

"Thank you, Mr. Coop!"

Practice continues on without Coop, and I can tell that he's torn between getting back to it or staying to say something else. He looks up at me and then back down. Then to Jim and then back to me. By this point a group of fans have gotten their nerve up to ask him for an autograph and so the drill begins.

I hand Jane a stack of photos and a Sharpie and tell her what to do. "You try it today, Jane."

She now stands in my usual spot and like the quick

learner she is, she hands Coop what he needs as he works through the line. It's just a small thing, but I enjoyed assisting with this part of the day. It brings so much joy to so many people just to have the opportunity to talk to a famous football player and get his autograph.

Now I'm sitting back and watching Jane take my place. Maybe it's silly, but I feel kind of melancholy about it. Slowly but surely, he doesn't need me anymore. Maybe he never did.

"Are you all right?" Jim asks.

"I should be asking you that. You're the one who was attacked by a football."

Jim chuckles. "I've been attacked by worse. Just out of curiosity, did you tell him what we talked about?"

I nod my head yes.

I realize that I gave Jim assurances that I would be discreet with the information he shared, and not go running off at the mouth, but Coop knows me too well. He could tell something was off. I had to spill the beans.

"I did."

Coop scribbles an autograph on a photo and turns to watch us talking. His eyebrows scrunch together.

"Owens, can I talk to you privately for a moment?"

"Are you finished signing?"

He quickly hands the photo to a young woman.

"Thank you for supporting us today." And then he turns his attention back to me.

"I'm done."

I walk with him to the side of the field. Our arms swinging side by side, almost touching, but not quite.

"Are you dating him?" he asks in an accusatory tone.

"I'm not sure that is any of your business."

"You work for me. That makes it my business."

"I work for you like five more days."

"He's a dick. I think he's trying to ruin my career."

"Is that why you tried to take his eye out with a football?"

"It was a mistake."

"You stink at lying."

"You two seem pretty close all of a sudden."

"Is this really what we should be discussing right now?"

"It's all I want to talk about."

"Well, I don't."

I turn to walk away, and he gently grabs my wrist.

"Where are you going? We're not done talking."

"I'm doing something that you've taught me recently. I'm ending a discussion without giving a rats ass if the other person was finished talking or not."

CHAPTER TWENTY-FIVE

COOP

"What are you doing?"

A pregnant woman holding two shopping bags approaches me. She looks very much like the woman I've seen in photos on Owens's bedroom wall. This must be her sister Carla.

"Just fixing a broken light," I assure her.

"You look more like you're breaking in the place."

"It does look a little suspicious doesn't it." I chuckle nervously.

"You're Cooper Barnes, I take it?"

"How did you know?" I grin. Hoping that my boyish charm will help melt the layer of ice coated around every word she says to me. I'm not sure this woman's heard anything good about me.

"Everyone in the city knows who you are. What they don't know is that you're also a handyman or maybe a cat burglar."

"Fixing things is one of my many hidden talents."

She gives me no more than a cursory once over.

"You're a lot hotter in person than you are on TV."

"Thanks ... I think."

"Does Ursula know that you're out here?"

"Probably not. I didn't want to disturb her."

"Interesting ... well it's a pleasure to finally meet you. I'm her sister Carla. I've heard a lot about you."

"Nice to finally meet you too, Carla."

"Is that your driver over there sitting in the car?"

"Yes."

"Tito, right?"

"How'd you know?"

"Ursula talks about him too. Ursula tells us *everything*. We're super close."

That was definitely some sort of warning.

"Tell him if he stays there too long that someone might call the cops on him. They don't like strange men sitting in cars on this block. Especially quiet men."

Carla sits her bags down on the ground and stretches out her back.

"I'm going to sit for a minute," she says.

So, I sit too.

"When's the baby due?"

"I've got about another three months. Why? Do I look like I'm about to drop?" She looks down at her belly. "Dexter keeps telling me to lay off the cookies."

"Dexter needs to mind his own business. You look great."

"Thanks, but this baby is kind of Dexter's business. He's the daddy."

"Still."

"Yeah, I guess you're right. *Still*, he should be nicer."

"Do you know what you're having?"

"Hopefully a sane human being."

I laugh at her joke. I'm starting to see where Owens gets her quick wit. Her sisters both have it too.

"Actually, I do know the sex of the baby, but I told my sisters that I didn't. I'm having a boy. I hope you can keep a secret."

"Congratulations, and yes I can keep a secret."

"Good. So now that we're getting to know each other a little better, I feel comfortable talking to you about something. About Ursula."

"Okay."

I glance up at Owens's window at the mention of

her name. I've been lurking around her lately trying to get up the nerve to finally finish the conversation that she started. In the office, at the new school, at practice —but I just haven't been able to find the words yet.

I had Tito drive me by the apartment tonight so that I could talk to her privately, but I ended up just taking a screwdriver out of the glove compartment and fixing a short in the light outside. I never rang the buzzer.

"I mean it's not just a coincidence that you're creeping around her apartment fixing stuff, is it?"

"This is not what it looks like."

"No, I get it. Her quitting kind of threw you for a loop. You might feel a little lost or angry even."

"Well—"

"But this is the thing, Coop. I hope I can call you that."

"Of course."

"I think you're probably a good guy. A little demanding and self-centered, but that's just because you've got money and all rich people are like that. So, that I can understand. But when it comes to Ursula ... working for you is just not good for her."

My face drops.

"I'm not trying to be a bitch or anything, but you have to understand. Ursula came to our family a broken little girl. She was in a horrible car accident that her mother died in. She had terrible nightmares for years after it. It affected every aspect of her life. Her sleeping. Her eating. Her self-confidence.

"We did everything we could to help her. To support her. She didn't have any friends at school, so we made her audition for the school plays, so that she would be forced into situations where she would have to interact with other kids. Something about being in those plays clicked for her, and she continued participating in the theater program all through high school and college.

"Now I'm not saying that we have a Meryl Streep or Angela Bassett on our hands, but I'm saying that there's a moment when she's on stage that the pain of her past slips away. That it's just her and the audience. And if that's where she can find her moments of peace, then that's what I want for her."

Carla's words rock me to the core. I'd always believed that I was doing the right thing by Owens, but maybe I haven't been. Maybe I've actually been the completely clueless narcissist that everyone thinks I am and made this all about me.

"So, you don't want her to work for me."

"At first, I thought it was insane for her to give up such a great position. God knows you pay her well and she gets to meet so many cool people. Travel places."

"But—"

"But I think you're confusing her."

"How?"

I'm not sure what Owens has told them and what she hasn't.

"What I'm saying is she's never going to follow her dreams working for you and ... falling in love with you. She is going to get hurt. You and I both know that. And that is something me and our entire family won't stand back and let happen."

"Fall in love with me?"

"I don't need my sister to tell me that she's falling for you. I can tell, and based on what I know about Ursula, it needs to end. You need to let her go."

"Things are a lot more complicated than they seem, Carla."

"What's complicated? You let her quit, and you let her go, and then you go live your big glamorous life. We'll take care of any collateral damage. There will be some but not as much as if you wait a year to break her heart."

"I'm not going to break her heart."

Wait ... will I?

"I'm asking you to let my sister go. Let her figure

out on her own how to fill her empty spaces. She's filled them with you for so long, she doesn't know anything different."

I just had an aha moment and it hurts something awful. Worse than any broken bone I've ever had.

"I understand what you're saying."

Carla stands up, lifting her shopping bags with her.

"It's been a pleasure meeting you, Coop. You're not as fucked up as I thought. You have a good life."

A painful smile reaches my eyes.

"Good luck with the baby."

Carla waits for me to get in the car and start driving before she rings the bell. She wants to make sure I'm gone. As we drive away, I can see Tito staring at me in the rearview mirror with a look on his face that I can't quite describe. If I had to give it a name, I'd say it was disappointment.

"What, Tito?"

"What are you going to do?"

Tito is the only person I've ever confided in about the little girl I pulled out of the car that day. I'm not sure why I told him. I guess I needed to tell someone, and I knew I could trust him with it.

"I'm going to go to the airport. I need to get away and get my head straight."

"You sure that's what you want to do?"

"I think I went about all of this the wrong way. Maybe I was doing this more for myself than for her. I've got to put Owens first for once."

"You've put her first for three years. You made good on your promise to her. You came back for her. You protected her. You made her strong. You love her, man. Anyone with half a brain can see that, or at least I see it."

I lean my head against the window as we move silently through the streets of Brooklyn. It feels heavy like my heart. Like there's nothing that I'll ever be able to do to lift it.

I miss her already.

COOP

A day that has been so painful for Owens that her subconscious chose to protect her from it wasn't the case for me. I can still smell the smoke. I can still see the fire. And I can still see the cars piled up on top of each other like mangled Legos. I always have.

The fact that Owens knows the truth or at least part of the truth scares me. The fact that she was staring at me like I'm some hero who saved her wrecks me. I'm nobody's hero. And actually, for a long time I thought I was a coward. A coward that allowed a middle-aged woman with red lipstick and large breasts to trick me into a car, then kidnap me, then frighten me. I hated myself for a long time over it.

The accident that stole Owens's mother gave me back my freedom, because I was also a part of that crash. The storm was coming down hard and fast and my kidnapper couldn't see well no matter how fast she increased the wiper speed. If she had been smart she would have pulled over until the rain passed, but she wasn't smart, she was desperate. Desperate to move me to a new location and take the place of her dead son. A son whom I later found out that she accidentally smothered.

Our car skidded into the car in front of us which held Owens and her mom. Sending their car spinning and toppling over to the side of road. Another car hit us from behind, and then another, and then another. The front of our car crunched like an accordion, trapping my kidnapper in her seat. I, on the other hand, was injured but able to free myself from the back.

I later discovered that my eardrum was punctured, but that I probably didn't feel much pain because of the adrenaline coursing through my body. I remember banging the back door with my fists. Frantically trying to free myself. I didn't know if the kidnapper could move or not. All I could hear were her muffled moans of pain and pleas for help. They fueled me. I wanted to get away from her as fast as I could. I hoped that she died in there.

Once I escaped, I did my best to hobble as quickly as I could to the wreckage. I didn't know who I'd find inside but discovered that it was a woman in front and a little girl unconscious in the back. Owens. I went to the woman first. She was hanging upside down, her breaths were shallow, and her eyes wide open. It was frightening at first.

"Help her," she whispered through what seemed like excruciating pain. "Help my daughter."

I used all of my strength left to open the back door of their car. Sliding out the girl I later learned to be Ursula Owens to the side of the road.

She was small, shivering, and at the time it seemed like the life was escaping her little body. Perhaps she was only in shock. I didn't know. I did the only thing that I could think to do. I covered her with my body. Shielding her from the rain until help arrived.

Soon I heard the sirens. They were still at a distance, but they were making their way toward us. I knew help was coming. Coming for me, for the girl, for her mom, and to arrest the horrid woman who took me.

But then I saw the car door jiggle. My kidnapper was trying to free herself, and I feared that she was getting really close to succeeding. I was frightened. There was no way I was going back with her. No way.

"Wake up." I tried shaking Owens awake. "Wake up, little girl."

When her eyes finally opened I was so relieved. Then I saw my captor nudging her car door open. Her beady eyes looking desperately for me.

She still couldn't get the door open enough to slide out, but I didn't know that at the time. I panicked. I had to get away. *I can leave the little girl here* I remember thinking. Help is on the way. She'll be fine. The woman wants me. A boy. Not a little girl.

"Sit here for a minute," I told her.

"My mommy," she pleaded.

She wanted me to go back and help get her mom out of the car. She didn't understand that I couldn't help even though I wanted to. I was only a kid myself. I couldn't carry a grown woman. I had barely gotten her out.

"One of the grown-ups will help her," I assured her. "I'm sorry, but I can't do it."

She began to cry.

"Wolf! Where are you, Wolf?"

I could hear my kidnapper calling for me. She was in pain. She was angry. It baffled me for days how she knew my family nickname—Wolf. I later learned that she had been watching me at the playground for days. And after that week as her captive, I never wanted to hear that nickname again.

"I gotta go," I told Owens. "The firemen are almost here. Don't worry. They'll get your mom out."

"Wait!"

"I'll come back for you, but I gotta go right now, okay? Sit right here. Don't move and they'll help you."

"Don't forget," she said before falling back into unconsciousness. "Don't forget to come back for me, Wolf."

CHAPTER TWENTY-SEVEN

URSULA

There's a heavy knock on my door. It startles me because that doesn't happen very often. I don't often talk to my neighbors because I'm never home and when I have a guest over, they have to be buzzed in the main door by me. I didn't buzz anyone in. I'm in pajamas and on the sofa watching *Charmed* reruns.

I open the door to find a contrite but beautiful man standing before me. It's Coop and it's only once I've opened the door that I realize how much I've missed him. I didn't go to work for the past few days because I was so angry at him, but at this moment, I don't care about any of that. All I want to do is hug him … but I don't.

"How did you get inside of my building?"

"A couple of nice ladies let me in."

"They just let you in huh?"

"Yep." He snaps his fingers. "Just like that."

"Of course … it's always so easy for you."

"You think anything about this is easy, Owens?"

"What do you mean *this*?"

"Can I come in?" he asks with a rich, bass heavy voice.

"I don't know. Are you in your right mind today?"

I open the door and allow him inside.

"Are you still worried about the guy who was willing to throw me under the bus and write about something private? Something I didn't want to share with the world."

"I didn't realize he threatened you with that information."

"He did."

"He doesn't seem that slimy."

"But he is."

"Okay, but he didn't write it."

"As far as you know."

"He promised me he wouldn't when he told me."

"Oh, right and because he promised that means it's true."

"I'm just saying that you didn't have to hit him with a football. There are legal options you can explore if he prints misinformation or—"

"It's not even really about what happened back then. He made it quite clear that he was interested in you. That he was going to pursue you. And it looked like ... it looked like that was happening."

"We were just talking like we do at any other practice, Coop. He's just a friend."

"Really—because you seem to be mighty concerned about his well being right now, and I don't particularly like that shit."

"I was worried for you not him. Hitting him with the ball was beneath you. You were embarrassing yourself."

"Well I'm not embarrassed by the shit at all. I'd do way more than hit somebody with a football for you, Owens. I would do any fucking thing."

"Coop—"

"You think you know what happened that day. You only know half of the story. Yes, I was abducted. Yes, it was us who crashed into your car ultimately killing your mother. Yes, it was me who pulled you out of that car, then left you on the side of the road."

"Coop—"

"I told them, Owens. I told anyone who would listen that you two needed help and went to you. The officers finally listened and took me back, but the ambulance was cutting your mother out of the car and they had you on a gurney. It looked like you were safe, so it was time for them to do their job and get me back to my family. I didn't think your mother would die. I swear to you. I didn't know."

"Thank you, Coop."

"But your mom."

"You're not responsible for her death. You didn't kill her. That insane woman who took you is responsible for that. That wasn't your fault. You have to know that."

"But I left you there."

"I never thought that. I don't think that. You pulled me out of the car and you comforted me when I was most afraid. That's more than most adults would have done."

"Your mom asked me to help, Owens. I need you to know that in those last moments, she was thinking of you. She must have loved you so much."

Tears start to fall. I know my mother loved me more than life itself, but hearing the words from the last person she said anything to really hits home.

"Thank you for telling me that."

He continues explaining himself. I know he needs to do it, and I want to hear everything he has to say, so I continue to stand patiently in front of him and listen to every word.

"Once I signed my first contract with the NFL, I knew that the very first thing I wanted to do with my money was to look for you. The little girl I made a promise to which I couldn't keep."

"You *did* keep it. You came back for me."

I won't allow him to keep saying that. He's distorted the truth. We're both survivors. Coop was a hero.

"It took me almost two years to find you, because like Jim told me once, no paper trail is ever truly destroyed. I can only describe it as kismet when I found you though. You had been out of school for three months and needed employment. I needed an assistant. I found your résumé on a basic job site by accident. I recognized the name from a copy of the police report that I'd gotten my hands on. I forwarded your application to the agency who was screening applicants for me."

My heart actually almost skips a beat.

I wasn't invisible like I thought.

I actually was important to him.

I've always been important.

"They must have thought you were an idiot passing on that pitiful résumé." I laugh.

"Nah, they were too busy thinking about all the babies they wanted to have with me to question my applicant selection."

I laugh. "Honestly, Coop, not every woman is attracted to you."

"Your sister couldn't catch her breath when she saw me in person at the bar and grill."

"She was acting like that because she was drunk and you're a celebrity, not because you're gorgeous."

"You think I'm gorgeous?"

He moves closer to me.

"I didn't say that ... exactly."

"I think you just did," he says in a voice dripping with want.

My eyes close and I practically melt when Coop cradles the side of my face with his hand.

"And you know what they say. Birds of a feather flock together. I think you're drop dead gorgeous too. Especially these big, brown eyes."

He kisses each of my eyelids softly.

First the left.

Then the right.

"And these soft lips."

He kisses each corner of my mouth until he coaxes it open. The kiss begins sweetly and crescendos in a passionate claiming of my mouth.

When he releases me from it, I am breathless.

I am forever changed.

That was an unforgettable kiss.

But he's not done with me.

Not by a long shot.

CHAPTER TWENTY-EIGHT

URSULA

Coop's hand starts to slide down my neck and trace my collarbone softly. Then he carefully works his fingertips farther down. "And your breasts."

I hold my breath as his fingers move deftly over my nipples. My breasts are relatively small, but my nipples are extremely sensitive to temperature and to touch. He kisses my neck as he continues to lightly tug on my right nipple.

I let out a small groan of pleasure.

"So fucking responsive."

Coop drops to his knees, and because of our height difference, his mouth comes directly face-to-face with my breasts. He quickly claims my left breast as he continues to manipulate the right nipple with his fingers.

I moan in delight.

While I have made out with other guys before, not one of them ever gave my breasts this much attention. I think because of their size, they were an afterthought to some, but Coop seems to like them. That makes me a lucky girl.

He blows a few warm breaths on my nipple and then switches maneuvers. Sucking the right and now playing with the left.

My eyes close in bliss, but when I do, it throws my equilibrium off for a moment. Before I topple over, Coop grabs me by my hips and holds me still. Now he alternates suckling at my breasts.

"I think everything about you is beautiful, Owens. The look of you. The smell of you. The taste of you."

He slides my sweatpants down gently and kisses my hip bones and my belly button. I start to grow nervous as he reaches my pubic hairline. That's been a no man zone my whole life. I tense up.

"Are you nervous?"

"Uh-uh," I lie.

"Do I have your permission to explore this beautiful body any further?"

"Yes." I grin.

"Have there been any explorers here before me?"

"Coop!" I laugh. "Who asks a question like that at a time like this?"

"This is the time to ask it. I need to know how slow I need to go, how careful I need to be, because right now I want to rip your clothes off and devour your cunt. I'm sure it's dripping for me by now."

I almost choke on my own saliva.

"I don't know how to answer that."

"Are you a virgin, Owens?"

"Yes."

He seems very pleased with that answer.

"I'll go slow then."

He slides my pants a bit down farther and slides a finger in between the folds and then into his mouth.

"You're soaking fucking wet."

I close my eyes in embarrassment.

Coop is so dirty.

"Eyes on me, darlin'."

I open them slowly.

He's grinning. Almost laughing.

"Do you think dirty thoughts about me when we're at the office? When you're watching me at practice? Are you wet like this all the time for me, Owens? You must be. You've been a very bad girl these last few years."

"Coop!"

"Should I continue?"

"I feel like I already said yes a thousand times already. Stop playing around."

"Just checking." He chuckles. "I don't want there to be any question that you were practically begging for it when you complain about how sore you are tomorrow."

"Saying yes is begging?"

He yanks my pants completely to the floor now and lifts each one of my legs out of them.

"There will be begging," he growls.

Still on his knees he pulls me closer to his mouth and begins sliding his tongue through my folds, the same place where his fingers have just been, directly against my clit. The feeling is exquisite.

"Coop," I say breathlessly.

The more I moan and say his name the more excited he becomes. Lapping at my sex faster and faster until my legs begin to shake like they have a mind of their own.

"Please!" I cry out.

Coop sits his butt back on his heels and pulls me so far on his face that I'm practically straddling his head. I hold on for dear life to the roots of his long strands with both hands.

I feel like I'm having an out of body experience as he continues to explore me with his tongue. Tears start to gather in the corners of my eyes as I can feel the start of a powerful orgasm beginning to build.

"I'm coming!" I scream as my entire body violently contracts and I see tiny flecks of light behind my eyelids.

He lifts my body and lays me gently on the floor in front of him and continues to lick and suck between my legs. I continue to have tiny orgasm aftershocks that make my head feel dizzy. When he finally lifts his head from between my legs, he has a ravenous look in his eyes that lets me know that this night is far from over.

"I told you there'd be begging."

It has only just begun.

CHAPTER TWENTY-NINE

COOP

In this moment if Owens asked me to buy her a mansion, build her a pool, and give her ten fucking babies I would. The sound of her coming made my dick harder than it's ever been. Her pussy tasted like nirvana. I can only imagine what it's going to feel like once I'm inside of it. I might lose my mind.

I give her a few moments to come down from her orgasm before I continue, but I'm like a kid in a candy store. I want to sample everything, and I want to have it now. It's all sweet to me.

I peel off my clothes as she breathes heavily watching my every move. It makes me feel like a fucking king the way she is staring at me. Her eyes are like two huge billboards flashing the message: *Please Give Me More.*

Message received.

I don't want her first time to be on her living room floor, so I scoop her up and carry her into her bedroom. Once inside, I lay her down on the bed and start kissing her again. This time slowing the tempo down. In between kisses I tell her dirty things, because that's what she does to me. That's how she makes me feel.

Filthy.

"Your pussy tastes like candy," I tell her.

She smiles.

"Can you taste it? It's all over my mouth."

I kiss her passionately.

"When I fuck you, your eyes are going to roll back inside of your head."

I slide one of my fingers between her folds as her hips squirm. She's dripping wet for me. Again. I make a mental note that my girl likes dirty talk.

I begin working my middle finger inside of her pussy. Getting her primed and ready for what's to come.

"Lift and wind your hips, Owens," I instruct her.

"Fuck my finger good. If you do a good job, I'll give you another one."

Like with any task, Owens can follow instructions like a motherfucker. She lifts and rotates her hips while I finger fuck the shit out of her. I slide another finger in to get her used to more girth.

After I catch a rhythm, I start to use my thumb to simultaneously rub her clit, and it doesn't take long for her pussy to start clamping around my finger like the greedy girl she is.

"That's right, baby," I encourage her. "You're about to come for me, aren't you?"

She whimpers a *yes* and it's the sweetest sound I think I've ever heard.

I'm just starting to learn how to expertly strum Owens's body, but I think I can tell that she's ready to blow, so I quickly pull my fingers out of her cunt and right when she lifts her hungry hips up for more—I slap her pussy hard.

Whack!

"Oh my God!" she screams as her body convulses for the second time tonight. This time I can watch her face as she orgasms, and revel in the beautiful mixture of pain and pleasure that clouds her expression.

"You want more? I ask her.

"Yes."

"Yes, what?"

"Yes, please."

Good girl, Owens.

"Like I said, there will be begging."

I claim one of her breasts with my mouth again enjoying the feeling of her squirming under me. I start trailing kisses back up along her neck, near her ear, and then to her mouth where I slide my tongue in and hungrily take what's mine. After a moment, I reluctantly pull away to look her in the eyes. I need to know that we're on the same page.

"Are you with me, baby?"

"Yes."

"I mean are you really with me?"

"Yes, I'm with you."

"This is going to hurt a little bit," I tell her. "But if you give me a second, then it's going to feel fantastic."

She nods her head.

"I trust you."

Three words that cut me to the core.

She trusts me.

I will never disappoint Owens again.

I swear my life on it.

I spread her legs apart and massage her clit again. Then I lift them on my shoulders and pull her ass farther down closer to me. I line myself up against her entrance and try not to overthink it. If I do, then this won't happen.

I'm horny, I'm nervous and I'm excited all rolled into one. I don't want to hurt her, but the only way this thing is going to work is for me to get it in there and start.

So, I start pushing and playing with one of her breasts as I hold my body above hers with my other arm. She bites her bottom lip a bit from what I think is the feeling of a lot of pressure. I'm a big boy. There's no getting around that. It will take some getting used to.

"Owens?" I hesitate.

"I want you, Coop," she says in an almost guttural voice. "Please don't stop."

"Okay, baby, here I come."

I continue pumping inside of her until I'm past her barrier and completely inside of her, and I swear I almost come in that very moment.

It's tight.

It's warm.

It's right the fuck where I want to be every second of the day if she will let me.

It's where I belong.

"You feel so fucking good," I say in between careful, sweaty, strokes.

"So do you," she moans in response as she lifts and winds her hips almost like she did when my finger was inside. Damn, she's a fast learner.

"I love this pussy," I profess. My voice growing stronger and more guttural. My orgasm slowly beginning to build. "Who does it belong to?"

She makes some sort of indescribable noise of pure pleasure, but I need the words. I've got to have them.

"Whose pussy is this?!" I demand to know again as I pump in and out of her harder and harder. Our sweaty bodies clapping together.

"I ... it's—"

She can't really talk ... which is probably a good thing ... but you know me ... so I give her a little push over the edge.

I slide my hand in between us and start stroking and pinching her clit as I pound inside of her harder. I might kill us both before she gives me the answer.

"Whose. Pussy. Is. This?!" I snarl.

And finally, I get what I need on the last stroke.

"Yours!" she cries out. "Yours!'

The contractions of her orgasm squeeze my dick like a vice, and we both come within seconds of each other. Her aftershocks continue to milk me completely dry, and then I fall on top of her completely spent.

"Wowza!" I say and start laughing.

"That's exactly what I was thinking." She laughs as she continues to breathe heavily.

Oops, I might be squishing her, so I lift myself off of her and fall over on the bed huffing beside her.

"Are you okay?"

"I'm better than okay."

"I know you don't like getting sweaty."

"Okay, but this time I did."

"So you liked it?"

"Yes, Coop. It was everything I hoped it'd be and best of all it was with someone who cares about me."

"Cares about you?"

"Yes ... I mean you do care about me, don't you?" she asks with some trepidation.

"Ursula, I don't just care about you. I love you. I think I always have. You are it for me. It's pretty clear now that you'll be stuck with me for much longer than you originally intended whether you quit your job or not."

Her eyes swell with tears. Shit, I think I may have fucked this up.

"Baby?"

"You called me Ursula."

"It's your name last time I checked."

"You never call me Ursula."

"Would you like me to never do it again? It did feel kind of weird."

"You can call me whatever you want."

She kisses my cheek.

"Then let's just stick with Owens."

I lift her hand and place a few small kisses on her knuckles.

"Coop?"

"Yes, baby."

"Can we do it again?"

CHAPTER THIRTY

URSULA

"Let's stay in bed."

"We can't. Wait. Coop. Ahh!"

Coop tosses me up and then I fall completely on top of him like a rag doll. Sometimes I don't think he realizes his own strength. Poor Jim had to ice his head when he got hit with that football for two days straight.

"Why not? Stay here on top of me and ride me into next week."

Coop has made it his life's mission to show me different sexual positions and then, of course, there's been "mandatory" practice sessions as well.

"We've played in bed every single night this week."

He looks at me with concerned eyes.

"You're right. I'm such a blockhead sometimes. Are you okay? You must be sore. We can keep it simple, and I can just eat you out tonight if you want. I'll lay you on the kitchen table and eat you like I'm at a buffet station."

"You're insatiable."

"Are you sick of me already?"

"It's not me that's the issue. It's you. You have to be exhausted. I know you, Coop. You need eight hours of sleep during training season."

"There's plenty of time for sleep when I'm dead. Spending my nights inside of you keeps me energized. It's the perfect cardio for my heart, baby. Fucking you doesn't make me tired. In fact, you're actually saving my life."

"I think you might just be certifiable considering how you just rationalized that."

"Should I prove to you just how much energy I have right now?"

I flip her over on her stomach and pretend that I'm going to take her doggy style. I look forward to doing that position again. I got so deep inside of her last night, that I put her pretty ass right to sleep two orgasms later.

"No! No!" She slaps me playfully. "I believe you."

"You know what? We're going out for the day. If we stay inside I'm going to want to kiss you, and touch you, and be inside of you—and I think you need a little break from all of this good loving."

"Oh brother."

"Come on, let's hit the showers."

"Together?"

"You're going to love it. There's plenty of things I can do in there that don't involve anything being inserted into your sore vagina."

I bet there are.

If there's one thing I'll give Coop when it comes to sex, it's straight As for creativity and a perfect score for execution.

I can't believe how the two of us have been spending the day together. I have Coop's complete attention. He barely looked at his phone all day, yet he miraculously seemed to have planned the perfect day.

First, we had a late brunch at a restaurant on the Upper West Side that I swear I've only mentioned once to Jane. You pick a main entrée and then you can choose from a dozen gourmet sides. All for one overinflated price. I had the crab cakes and Coop had the steak. It was scrumptious.

Next up was a visit to the Natural Sciences Museum to see an exhibit on Australia. A continent I'm dying to visit. I'm not sure how Coop knows that. I guess he was paying attention to some of the decorations in my room. The exhibition took us inside the Australian experience. Meeting its people, exploring its landscapes, and encountering its rare and unusual species. I think we both felt a little smarter after we finished our tour.

Now we're walking around downtown at a late night Arts in the Park Festival. There are artisans with tables all up and down ten city blocks featuring their wares. There are local bands playing music and food trucks too. Coop grabs my hand as we continue walking and stopping to look at different vendors. We look like a real couple. We feel like a real couple. It feels almost surreal. One minute I couldn't wait to get away from him, and now I don't think I ever want to leave him again.

"I can't wait for you to meet my whole family, Coop."

"I'd like that. It's not fair that you've met my parents and I haven't met your dad and Evelyn."

"Well you have at least met Monica already."

"Yeah, but I think I should meet her sober."

"Well she pretty much acts the same drunk or sober."

I chuckle. "Sounds like a fun girl."

"She is and so is Carla even though she's pregnant."

"Actually, Carla and I have already met."

"When was that?"

"It might have been one of the days I was sniffing behind you like a puppy dog and she caught me."

"What does that mean? You're not making sense."

"She and I met outside of your apartment not too long ago."

"Why am I just hearing about it now? Why didn't she mention it?"

"She asked me to let you go, Owens, and I actually considered it for a moment. The chickenshit part of me was ready to use what she said as an excuse not to be real with you. But then I manned up and the rest is history. Here we are.

"But I need you to know that just because we're together now doesn't mean you can't go pursue whatever it is you want. In fact, I want you to quit being my assistant. Go be an actress. Go start a business. Do whatever you want. I will help you and support you in any way I can."

"I've been thinking about things a lot over the last few days, and I don't think that I want to leave."

"What do you mean?"

"There's not one day that I've woken up in the last three years and said to myself that I missed being on stage. Not one. I wanted to leave this job and pursue acting because I thought that I was supposed to, because that's what everyone expected me to do, because that's what my mom did. I felt like I was disappointing my family if I didn't. But truth be told, I really like what I do, and I'm good at it. So as long as you're on board, I really want to stay. Plus, I think you need me."

"I definitely need you."

"And I think there's enough work for us to do that you can keep both me and Jane on."

"Are you sure? I have some pretty good contacts in Hollywood. Favors I can call in."

"She got you good, didn't she?" I laugh.

"Who, your sister? Yeah, she's a tough lady."

"That's one way of putting it," I say understanding the persuasiveness of my sister better than anyone.

"Let's just say that she made me see things in a different light. I don't want to hold you back. Ever. And I won't. So, when I see her again, I'm going to reassure her of that. I'm going to win her over—"

"You don't have to worry about her. I've been handling her my entire life. I'm not going to let her give orders to the man I love like she's got some authority over–"

"Wait ... you love me, Owens?"

Coop stops and lifts me up a foot off of the ground, sliding me down against his body, and then kissing me before I can even respond.

"Say it again."

"I love you," I affirm my declaration.

"I love you too."

He whispers his confession softly in my mouth.

"You better."

I wrap my hands around his neck and slide them in the back of his hair.

"If somebody keeps touching me like that, she's going to *get it* behind one of these food trucks."

"You wouldn't dare!"

"I'm all about a dare, Owens."

"How about a funnel cake instead?" I say wiggling my eyebrows. "There are children afoot."

"I'm not eating any white sugar or white flour, babe. Plus, I'd rather eat you instead of a funnel cake any day. I'll give you a ten second start before I catch you. When I do, I'm pulling you behind a truck whether children are *afoot* or not."

"Coop!" I say in disbelief. "You better not."

"Ten, nine, eight—"

He starts counting and I start running.

"You're crazy!" I yell behind me. Laughing the entire time, I'm bobbing and weaving through the dozens of innocent festival shoppers.

"Good thing you're wearing your sneaks today," he yells in the crowd. "But too bad they're not going to save you. Here I come!"

CHAPTER THIRTY-ONE

URSULA

Whitehaven Beach
Whitsunday Island, Australia.

I am lying on crystal white silica sand, with my head on the chest of the man I love as we stare at the turquoise waters of Whitehaven Beach on the beautiful continent of Australia.

Evidently cross country travel is a perk of the job. Coop says this trip is especially for assistant appreciation day (totally made-up) and to celebrate the actual third year anniversary of the day I started working for him.

"I'm starving, Owens."

"You're always hungry."

"We haven't eaten in hours."

"All right, I guess the sun is going down."

"We'll do more beach tomorrow."

The nice thing about this trip is that we have a guide who has been taking care of us the entire time. He's ready to move at the drop of a dime and now he's whisking us off to another location farther around the island via boat.

When we arrive to our destination there is a beautiful white gazebo with a candlelight dinner for two waiting and an array of fresh plucked blooms are strewn about the floor and table.

"Happy Anniversary."

A man dressed in all white is standing on the side of the gazebo with a rolling cart of food and beverages. He begins to bring things to the table as Coop pulls out my chair for me.

"Sit."

I am grinning from ear to ear at this point because while Coop has been doing some sweet things for me since we've gotten together, this is hands down the most romantic.

He shocks me for a moment when he doesn't go sit across me but instead drops to his knees in front of me.

"Owens, I thought we'd always be comfortably in

each other's lives, but when you said the words *I quit,* that's when I realized that I could never let you go. That was the day that I realized, and fought at first, that from the very beginning you were the only one for me. I love you. Will you marry me?"

Under a strategically placed napkin on the table is a ring box. Coop pops it open and looks at me with a hopeful expression. The glare from the diamond almost blinds me. It's gigantic. Honestly, it's way too big, but I will never tell him that, because that's just a testament to Coop's heart.

Way too big.

"I'm not sure how you manage to still surprise me, but you do."

"That's not an answer."

I start taking off my mother's emerald ring, my good luck charm, and switch it to my other hand. I've got a new one now.

"I always knew that you were a fierce competitor, intelligent, and ridiculously funny. Now I know that you are also protective, serious, warm and loving. You are the only man I will ever love, Coop. Of course, the answer is yes."

Coop slides my new, big, fat, gaudy diamond ring on my finger and the tears start to fall. I never imagined for one second that I'd be in love and now marrying my boss. The boy who saved me. The man who loves me.

Then we kiss.

Madly. Passionately.

And it's even better than the first time we did it, because this time I was sober, but more importantly this time I know without a shadow of a doubt that the kiss means he will always come back for me.

Four Years Later

"Congratulations to the first graduating class of Brooklyn Summit Preparatory High School For Boys!"

The applause intensifies to a thunderous roar as a group of one hundred boys of all shapes and sizes stand in their solid blue uniforms, beaming with pride. They've completed four years of a rigorous program that we all hope has set them up for success. The proudest one of them all though is their benefactor and my loving husband.

"You've done a good thing with these boys, Coop."

"Congratulations, Cooper."

"You must be so proud, Mr. Barnes."

Everyone is congratulating my husband for a job well done and he deserves every bit of the praise. He had a vision and a determination to make this school the gold standard for what he hopes will be many more schools to follow.

"Raise the bar high and watch a child lift their hands to reach it."

The boys repeat the school's motto in unison.

The crowd applauds again.

"This was an amazing *extravaganza* wasn't it?" I smile as I lean into Coop. "How do you feel?" I ask him as we stand next to each other in a faculty receiving line. Shaking the hands of the graduates as they leave the Kirtrina Owens Auditorium, named after my mother.

"It's a cross between our wedding day and the first time I scored a touchdown."

"Wowza! Then that's good."

"Exactly."

"I wonder if I could top that though?"

"You top that most nights," he whispers in his deep, baritone voice that I've grown to crave.

"Yeah, but I think you're going to feel even prouder when our own son walks across that stage."

"Yeah, that will be ... wait ... what do you mean *our* son?"

"We're having a baby," I say excitedly.

"What! You literally stopped taking the pill like yesterday."

"More like two months ago. I took the test this morning. You were so preoccupied with graduation this morning, I wanted to wait to tell you."

He places his large palm against my stomach. Then bends over to whisper in my ear.

"Even my sperm move fast like me," he says using a mock tone of awe in his voice. "I am spectacular at all things."

"That you are, husband. That you are."

I laugh so hard that my stomach grows queasy. It's funny how Carla never mentioned how morning sickness is really all day sickness. I guess once she gave birth to Little D, she conveniently forgot about all of that. I can't believe that he'll already be starting kindergarten in the fall, and soon he'll have a little cousin to play with and protect.

I'm so happy.

And the great thing about it is, I will easily be able to bring my child to work once he or she is born.

Because I definitely don't think the boss will mind.

Wolf was a sexy and intense loner full of secrets, but **Diesel** is the best friend and boy next door who got away.

Two best friends. One hot romance. Lots of obstacles. Will these two childhood sweethearts find their way back into each other's hearts and lives or will they keep repeating the same mistakes?

Read this sweet and sexy **friends to lovers** sports romance today.

TAP TO DOWNLOAD DIESEL NOW

The Masterson Series

Devour this addictive series about the possessive bad boy, Roman Masterson, who falls hard and fast for the girl he's promised his family to protect.

Masterson

Masterson Unleashed

Masterson In Love

Masterson Made

Joseph Loves Juliette

The King Brothers Series

Dive into this series of interconnected standalones featuring 3 alpha hot brothers and the women they lay claim to without apology.

Claimed - Camden & Jade

Indebted - Cutter & Sloan

Broken - Stone & Tiny

Promised - All King Brothers

The Nighthawk Series

Sexy & sweet sports romances set in the professional world of football. All standalones.

Saint - Saint & Sabrina

Wolf - Cooper & Ursula

Diesel - Mason & Olivia

Jett - Jett & Adrienne

Rush - Rush & Mia

The Valencia Mafia Series

Coming Soon. Get Notified!

WHERE YOU CAN FIND ME

MY VIP LIST (Get the nitty gritty)

I have a VIP Reader mailing list. I only send free books, new release, sales or special giveaway info to this group. No spam. Please join here:
http://LisaLangBlakeney.com/VIP

MY PRIVATE FAN GROUP (Casual fun)

Join my private Fan Group on Facebook also known as my "Romance Ninja Warriors" where I share all things new going on, celebrate birthdays, post teasers, yummy pics, giveaways and just chit chat.
http://LisaLangBlakeney.com/community

ACKNOWLEDGMENTS

I'm sorry I didn't cook…

Thank you to my husband and my daughters for understanding that microwaves were invented for a reason. Love you madly.

I'm sorry I couldn't talk…

Thank you to my loyal group of friends who now understand that "I'm On Deadline" means that I can't shoot the shit tonight.

I'm sorry it was late…

Thank you to editor Marla Esposito who I just adore and who understands and accepts when I send her chapters out of order and on different days.

And a special thanks...

To all of the readers and authors who have supported me in any way during my author journey. You all are amazing!

xoxo,

Lisa

ABOUT THE AUTHOR

Lisa Lang Blakeney is an international bestselling author of contemporary romance sold in more than 28 countries. Worried that her fellow PTO moms might disapprove, she wrote and published her steamy debut novel Masterson under a different title and pen name in August of 2015.

Thanks to strong reader support of her alpha male character, Roman Masterson, she was encouraged to continue with the series and published the entire Masterson Trilogy the following year. She hasn't looked back since and continues to write novels featuring strong alpha men and the smart women they seek to claim.

A romance junkie for sure, you can find Lisa watching a romantic comedy, reading a romance novel, or writing one of her own most days of the week. If she's not doing that, she's outside in the garden tending to her roses.

Lisa is the wife of one alpha (whom she met in college), mother to four girls, and two labradoodles. Get news on releases, sales and giveaways when you become one of Lisa's VIP readers at : http://LisaLangBlakeney.com/VIP

You can also get text notifications and never miss a new release when you text the words **always alpha romance** to 31996

facebook.com/authorlisalangblakeney

twitter.com/LisaLangWrites

instagram.com/LisaLangBlakeney

amazon.com/author/lisalangblakeney

bookbub.com/authors/lisa-lang-blakeney

goodreads.com/Lisa_Lang_Blakeney

pinterest.com/lisalangwrites